Vet Nurse to the Rescue

by Donna Harris
Illustrated by Abigail Banks

© **Donna Harris 2020**

Illustrated by Abigail Banks

ISBN 978-0-9931802-6-2

Typeset by Oxford eBooks
www.oxford-ebooks.com

Contents

Acknowledgements

I would like to thank Benjamin Mee who had rescued Dartmoor Zoo after it had been forced to close. Benjamin then donated the zoo to the Dartmoor Zoological Society which is a charity. Without his passion for the wildlife in his care, I may never have had the opportunity to use my radiography skills on these stunning creatures. I would thoroughly recommend anyone to visit the zoo and support the variety of wildlife there. Also my thanks go to South Moor Vets for supporting me through my Equine Nursing Certificate, and allowing me to follow my keen interest in large animal radiography.

Dedication

I would like to dedicate this book to all my friends who have been there for me throughout my career journey. Also for my loving Labradors Echo, Bumble and Eryn, who have passed away and will be forever in my memory.

Chapter One

Grace the orphan foal was getting stronger by the day, she was now four weeks old. Minty the lamb had provided the company she needed, and the two would curl up sleeping together, it was a wonderful sight.

Elly had been given the foal by the owner of the stud farm who bred her, together with her friend Lilly, they had taken on the enormous task of caring for the foal which couldn't stand alone without splints.

Elly changed the plaster cast splints twice a day, Grace was growing so fast, and she could see that the splints were starting to rub on her delicate fetlocks. Plenty of soft padding and cotton wool had been used under the splints to avoid pressure sores, but with Grace's growth it was not possible to use much padding as it was too bulky. The splints were open on the outside and were removed each time by stretching them apart, having to use both hands, whilst Grace lay there.

It was as if she knew she had to stay still. Elly would gently massage Grace's tiny fetlocks, smoothing and giving gentle physiotherapy to help strengthen the tendons and ligaments, and it would help get the blood circulation flow to her lower limb too. Grace was still unable to stand without the splints on, and Elly knew it was going to be a race against time, before she outgrew the splints.

Elly and Lilly had a lot of support from family and friends, who would do one of their night shifts for them, so that they managed a full nights sleep. The girls were able to work on a three hourly feeding shift. Two bottles at a time with both Grace and Minty sucking from a bottle each in the middle of the night, made it worth getting up for. Both had such lovely characters, the girls would sit in the corner of the stable, watching and cuddling the orphans. It may have been just cupboard love, but the young babies were always pleased to see them at feeding time.

"I am worried about the small sores appearing on Grace's fetlocks." Elly was explaining to Steve her boss whilst in the surgery.

Steve had popped in to check on Grace from time to time, to make sure of her well-being, and to ensure that Elly and Lilly were not fighting a losing battle.

"I will pop down to have a look next time you are doing a splint change." Steve said, and they arranged to meet at the stables that afternoon.

When Steve arrived at the stables he was pleased to see Grace standing with her splints on, she had soon strengthened up on her hind legs, which Elly had been bandaging for support daily. Steve checked Grace's hind legs first, and agreed that Elly could now leave the bandages off, and just concentrate on the forelegs. They changed the splints together, and Steve could see why Elly was worried. Grace had a small pressure sore on the lateral (outer) side of her fetlock. Elly had tried to add extra padding, but the splints were becoming tighter as Grace grew.

"I will give Grace some antibiotics, there is always a risk using antibiotics in a foal, but we have no option. I would recommend that you can only use the splints for another week. After that they must come off completely. You have both done really well and worked hard, but it would not be fair to let her suffer." Steve added "Carry on with the regular splint changes and physiotherapy, she is looking well in herself, and has good company with Minty."

Elly reported back to Lilly, the girls both found hidden energy and the strength to carry on with the intensive care that Grace needed. They both agreed to give Grace a deadline of a week. She had come on so far, from being that recumbent foal, that had laid helpless in the huge stable of straw, when they had first seen her to now, being able to skip around the stable with her splints on, having a game of hide and seek with Minty. The young lamb would dive for cover behind the water butt, that was in their stable if Grace got too frisky.

"I am going to try taking one of the splints off and just use a support bandage, on the leg with the sore."

Lilly looked at Elly and there were tears in her eyes, both girls knew it was Grace's only chance of survival; they had to get the splints off.

"OK." replied Lilly, "I can stay with Grace this afternoon and watch her, and help Grace up if necessary."

Elly removed the splint on Grace's left foreleg, and repeated her gentle massage of the leg. She then replaced the splint with a support bandage, being very careful with the fetlock sore, changing the dressing and cleaning the small wound that had appeared. It was difficult to support the fetlock without putting any pressure on the wound. But the use of a ring of cotton wool, known as a doughnut ring, provides a barrier. At least it would be less rigid than the plaster cast, and more comfortable for Grace when she stood up.

It was heartbreaking for the girls to watch as Grace tried to stand, she would knuckle over on the leg without the splint. But it had to happen, as she had virtually outgrown the splints.

"We will put the splint back on just for the middle of the night, when we are not here to watch her. I have got to get back to work now, I will come back in a couple of hours and take over from you." Elly explained to Lilly.

Lilly spent the afternoon watching over Grace. Each time Grace wanted to stand, Lilly was there to support her. When Elly arrived back to the stable she filled Elly in with details of how Grace had progressed.

"Once she is up she can walk around, it is just getting up, she knuckles over and stumbles."

Minty was confused, they couldn't take him out of the stable as he was there to be company for Grace, and the two had become inseparable.

Elly took over from Lilly, and she stayed to support Grace as she wanted to get up and down. Preventing Grace from damaging her head, as she occasionally stumbled around the stable was important. As much human support as possible was necessary, if Grace was going to survive.

Chapter Two

Elly had been house sitting for friends of hers in a beautiful old farm house close to the estuary and beach known as Wonwell. She was looking after an old hunter mare called Folly, along with two Labradors Roly and Bea.

The owners of the farm house were away, and it suited Elly to take the opportunity to get her own old cottage refurbished whilst she had somewhere else to stay. She also took her own two Labradors Bumble and Eryn. It was getting towards the end of summer in late August, and the farm was surrounded by barley fields which were almost ripe and ready for harvest cutting. Elly would take the dogs down the lane for a walk on the beach every morning. Although Roly was getting old and slow, he had to stay at home. Both Bumble and Bea were the same age, now six, and needed plenty of exercise. The beach walk was an ideal place to take them, where they could take a swim in the sea which they adored.

In the late afternoons, Elly would ride out Folly the old hunter mare, gradually getting her fit for her owner to ride her again. Mainly walking and trotting the lanes, with the occasional short canter. The scenery was stunning, and horseback was a good way to explore the countryside.

After riding, Elly sat in the garden with the dogs by her side. They were all laid out enjoying a snooze. Then, without warning a rabbit hopped out of the hedge in front of the dogs and headed towards the barley fields. Bea picked up the scent and immediately hot footed it into the field where the rabbit had gone.

"Oh no come back Bea, come back!" Ellie shouted.

She managed to grab Eryn and Roly, but missed catching

Bumble, who also hot footed it into the fields. "No, not you too Bumble come back." she shouted.

With quick thinking she put both Eryn and Roly into the house, and went to the edge of the barley field.

"Come on girls, Bumble, Bea come back good girls come back." she started to shout and get louder "Bea, Bumble!" her voice was getting croaky.

Oh no, she thought, what shall I do? Hopefully they will come back, but Elly was worried that one side of the barley field was alongside a busy lane, where holiday makers would be heading back from the beach. She took the decision to leave the farm and head up to the top road. She knew she had to have a look.

It didn't take long for Elly to edge the top of the field, she asked a couple of passing cars if they had seen two black Labradors.

"No sorry love, haven't seen any" replied one of the drivers.

Elly walked the edge of the field, she didn't want to call the dogs and encourage them to the road, if they were going to head back home then that would be ideal. She drove back to the farm and stood by the spot where they had entered the barley field. She called again, but it seemed to be in vain. I know, she thought, maybe I can stand high on something and see if the barley is moving and I can spot where they are?

She found a large wooden mounting block and dragged it to the side of the field. Climbing high on top of it she was able to see at least part of the field. But sadly no movement. By now Elly was getting upset. She had shouted and shouted until her throat was sore. She had to find the dogs.

"Bumble, Bea, where are you come on, come back please!!"

It would be dark in an hour, and she knew that black dogs on a country lane at night was an accident waiting to happen. She headed back up to the top road. Parking in a gateway.

Elly stopped several cars again. Then fortunately one replied "Yes, we have just seen them heading this way, they are panting a lot and looked lost but we couldn't get near them." the gentleman smiled at Elly and went on his way.

As soon as the car had driven off the two Labradors appeared. Elly was relieved, she caught them and praised them for coming back. She couldn't be tough on them as they didn't know how naughty they had been. But Elly was horrified with their faces. They must have gotten lost in the barley field and both their faces were swollen and they could hardly open their eyes.

"Oh no, you poor things, what has happened to you?" Elly put the dogs in the car.

Thinking fast she knew they needed help. The swelling could get worse and the pain must be horrid for them. She gave them both some water which she had already in the car, and drove straight down to where one of the vets lived at Ringmore a village close by.

Fortunately Elly found PK the veterinary at home.

"Gosh they are in the wars, looks like they have both been in a boxing match!" exclaimed PK.

He acted quickly, and went straight to the back of his Landrover truck and drew up two injections. They were of potent antibiotics and steroid injections which would take the sting out of the damage they had done to their faces.

Both Bea and Bumble were too sore to move far. And didn't object to the injections they were given.

"I will get Amy to make you a cuppa, and we can keep them under observation for an hour or so, to make sure they don't get worse."

PK invited Elly into the garden where they sat in the shade with the dogs, whilst Amy made Elly a welcome cup of coffee and also brought out some cake for them to share. Bea and Bumble were given plenty of water, and they soon settled down for a snooze.

Elly stayed for an hour before heading back to the house. "Thank you so much, hopefully one day I will be able to repay the favour, I'm sorry to disturb your evening."

"No problem." PK and Amy gave Elly a hug before she left. "You had better bring them both into the surgery tomorrow morning and I can check they haven't damaged their eyes."

Elly was grateful, she was relieved that not only had she found both dogs, but they hadn't been knocked over by a car in the busy lane, nor hopefully would there be long term damage to their eyes, thanks to the swift treatment from PK.

Chapter Three

Dartmoor Zoo was situated four miles from the surgery where Elly worked. It was full of exotic animals, and the veterinary work there was mainly covered by the Ivybridge branch surgery which was closer. One morning a phone call came from Will, one of the Ivybridge Vets.

"Elly I am trying to organise some x-rays to be taken of Blotch, one of the tigers at the zoo, he is really poorly. Can you make it this Thursday morning?" he asked.

"That sounds exciting, yes of course, what time would you like me there?" she replied.

"Don't get too excited, x-raying tigers is a dangerous job. I have a specialist coming down to look at the radiographs we take, so that we can treat Blotch whilst he is under anaesthetic." Will explained, he continued "Can you make it at 10am? We have to have a health and safety meeting first."

Blotch the tiger was only six years old, the zoo had tried treating him with supplements with his food, and the vets had also tried some electrolytes and supplements in his water. His health was gradually deteriorating and his illness needed further investigation.

Elly was still excited, not only to get a visit to the zoo, but also to get close up to the tigers and demonstrate her radiography skills, which had become part of her daily routine in her work.

On the morning of the visit, Elly checked that she had all the equipment in her car before travelling to the Zoo. x-ray generator, the large processor, x-ray plates, laptop, metal holders and stand, lead gowns, gloves and monitors for her and Will. It would be disastrous if she had forgotten anything. The magic of having all the equipment to hand is that the radiographs would be developed there and then for the specialist to look at the pictures straight away.

The team had assembled in the cafe at the zoo for the briefing. A marksman to heavily sedate the tiger, vets to anaesthetise him, zoo keepers, and the specialist zoo vet. They sat around the table with a cup of coffee reading through the health and safety regulations and then once they understood the importance, signing to say that they have read the terms and conditions. It was at this stage Elly gulped at the thought of the dangers involved. Then out of the corner of her eye, she noticed another zookeeper join the table.

"Sorry I am late." he apologised to the team.

The chap was in his thirties, had dark hair and a friendly face. Elly was pleased of the distraction. The gentleman then directed the team up to the tiger pen. Elly had to drive there and park next to the pen as she had the equipment in her car which needed an electricity source close by.

She heard both the roar of lions and tigers as she drove through the large pens. It was exciting, but still fearful. The tigresses in Blotches pen had been shut into individual stalls, both for their safety and for the safety of the team. Elly parked her car close by the pens, and unloaded her equipment ready for use. She and the team then waited patiently whilst the marksman stalked the tiger from outside the pen to dart him with the heavy tranquilliser. Blotch had been suspicious of the group of people and hid mainly behind the trees and shrubs in his pen, making it difficult for the marksman to get a clear shot.

Whilst the marksman was taking his time, the young chap who had appeared late at the meeting introduced himself to Elly.

"Hi I'm Benjamin, would you like to come and see the tigers in the stalls?"

Elly blushed, "Yes I would love to."

Benjamin led her into the enclosure where there were three female tigers in individual pens.

"Here you go, try this and she will lick your hand like a cat." Benjamin demonstrated by placing his hand flat against the strong wire mesh and the female tigress licked his hand.

"That's amazing." Elly replied and tried doing the same, with the tigress licking her hand too. "Thank you so much." she added.

With that, the call from the team came from outside that the tiger had been darted and was starting to fall asleep. They acted quickly and once Blotch was on the floor and appeared asleep, the strong zoo handlers carried him over to the sheet which had become their bed for him. Elly acted quickly too, she helped by carrying her equipment being the protective gowns which she gave to the immediate team close to Blotch, the x-ray stand and generator to the sheet which was just inside the pen gate. The team then thought it better to use one of the empty pens within the row just in case Blotch woke up, they could keep him close without him escaping back behind the trees. She had also taken along an Oxygen cylinder and mask which the vets would use on the tiger. The vets made sure Blotch was immobile enough for the radiographs to be taken by topping up his anaesthetic. Although it was scary, the job had to be done as quickly as possible to prevent any risk to Blotch's health and the health and safety of the team. The pressure was on. One by one the radiographs were taken, and Elly developed them in the processor in the back of her car and transferred the images onto the laptop for the vets to make their diagnosis. Once all the images had been taken, Elly transferred them onto a CD so that they could be looked at by another specialist at London Zoo for a second opinion.

Elly tidied up her equipment and replaced it all back in the car. The zoo team were happy that the job had been done without injury to any person. The vets had their worries about what they had seen on the radiographs but were going to wait for another specialist's opinion. Blotch was given some more medication by injections, before being given his anaesthetic reversal so that he could wake up.

Arriving back at the Ivybridge surgery, Caroline the branch manager asked "How did you get on Elly?"

"Wow it was amazing, not only to go to the zoo, but to see the beautiful wild animals there. We got the job done in a couple of hours, and hopefully now Blotch can get some supportive treatment." she continued "Oh and there was this really lovely zoo keeper there who showed me the tigresses who would lick your hand through the wire."

"Don't you know who that is Elly?" Caroline asked.

"No I haven't got a clue but he was really nice." Elly blushed

"That's Benjamin who owns the zoo, he wrote the book 'I bought A Zoo' and it was a famous film with Matt Damon in it!"

Chapter Four

Wildlife creatures come in all shapes and sizes, and not only did the practice treat the tigers and zoo animals, but were also open to treat any wildlife as immediate care which is brought into the surgery, for no charge.

It was the end of a long hot summer, and towards the end of the day, just before the vets and staff were closing up, a lady rushed in with a cardboard box.

"What do you have in there?" asked Elly.

"It's a hedgehog, we found it curled up in the middle of the road, maybe it was just scared but we didn't want it run over." the lady replied.

Elly asked the lady to take a seat whilst she took the box with the hedgehog in it to one of the vets who was sitting in a consult room.

"What do you have there then?" asked PK.

"It's a poorly hedgehog which a lady has just brought into us for a look at, she said he was found just curled up in the road." Elly replied.

"If you can go and find me the leather gauntlets which are down the back I will have a look." asked PK.

Elly headed off to find the leather gauntlets which were ideal for handling either animals which may bite, or ones which have prickly hairs like this particular hedgehog.

With the gauntlets on, PK was able to examine the hedgehog. Although with fear it was curled in a ball, he was able to get a stethoscope to listen to its heart rate.

"It's about 220 beats per minute, which I believe is normal. Maybe he is just dehydrated in this hot weather. We can take him in and give him some fluids, after which we will try and get him to the Prickly Ball Hedgehog sanctuary, if they will take it." he added "Elly you take him down the back and prepare some Selective rehydration recovery feed which we have a box of on the shelf, and I will talk to the lady in the waiting room."

It was the part of working in a mixed animal vet practice which Elly loved. Although her main interest was in horses and radiography, she would be happy to care for any creature which needed help.

"Hi there, my name is PK, thank you for bringing in the hedgehog."

The lady replied "Hello, I'm Mrs Walker, we found it in the middle of the road and couldn't just leave it there."

"Yes thank you for bringing him in, I identified it's a little boy. I think he is just dehydrated, we can give him some rehydration therapy here and then get him to the Prickly Ball sanctuary." he added obviously there is no charge to treat him here, but are you able to take him to the sanctuary for us please?"

"Sorry, I am late to pick my child up from his piano lesson, but thank you for seeing the hedgehog." Mrs Walker replied and left the surgery.

PK found Elly in the prep room making up the rehydration therapy.

"I have phoned Prickly Ball Farm and they are happy to take the hedgehog, but we need to get him there." he explained.

Elly replied "I will take him, I would love to see the sanctuary, it sounds fun."

They both gently dosed the hedgehog with the fluid by mouth, which he took readily.

"I think he will be fine, I will go and write up his notes Elly, he needs a name, what shall we call him?" PK asked.

"How about Horatio? As he is a hero if he survives, he

could easily have been squashed by a car." Elly smiled at the thought of Horatio surviving against the odds.

Once rehydrated Elly headed off on the ten mile trip to Prickly Ball farm sanctuary, where she would hand over Horatio for further intensive care. Before this day she had no idea that the farm existed, and was delighted to be shown around when she got there. The place was charity based, and had become a lovely theme park for families.

"Thank you for bringing Horatio in, he looks like we can help him in recovery, and well done for giving him some rehydration therapy before you brought him up to us. It could well have saved his life." explained Sarah the manager

With that she weighed him.

"He is only 400 grams, but he could be just young, the ideal weight for a hedgehog is 600 grams." Sarah said and added "I will put him in a cage in his box and give you a quick guided tour if you would like one?"

Elly was shown around the farm, there must have been about thirty hedgehogs in there, some in groups and some on their own under heat lamps.

Sarah told Elly "We rely on volunteers, I run the place and have a group of four volunteers who help out. We have open days for families which help raise funds as we are charity based and have to pay rent on the farm to the landowner."

"You have a great place here which I never knew existed, we are happy to promote your work in the surgery and take a poster for our notice board. Do let me know how Horatio gets on and thanks again." replied Elly as she left the farm for Sarah to attend to Horatio and the other hedgehogs in her care.

The follow up news on Horatio was good. He responded to the rehydration therapy and after he put on weight in two weeks he was released back into the wild.

Chapter Five

No day was ever the same in the surgery. It made for a very interesting life for Elly, and this particular day would be one that stuck strongly in her mind. She received a phone call from one of the vets Julie.

"Hi Elly, I need you to help me, can you get away from the surgery?" asked Julie.

"Yes, I am just here typing up worksheets; there are plenty of staff around, what's up?" Elly asked.

"Well you know on my visit list, there was a call to cleanse a cow for Mrs Spencer at her farm. Well she has had a fall, but I have a list of other calls which I need to get onto. Are you able to take her to the health centre to get her checked over please?" asked Julie.

"Yes of course, I will come up now." Elly replied. She liked any excuse to get out in the fresh air, but she had no idea how bizarre the day would turn out.

Elly arrived at the farm to be welcomed by Mrs Spencer who was in her 80s and was holding her arm obviously in some pain.

"What have you been up to?" Elly asked.

"Oh it's nothing dear, thank you for collecting me. I am sure I could drive but Julie the vet insisted she asked you."

"It's no problem, I am pleased for any excuse for some fresh air." replied Elly and they headed down to the surgery which was only two miles away.

Elly walked into the health centre with Mrs Spencer and headed towards the reception desk.

"This is Mrs Spencer, she has had a fall at her yard. I can see there may be a bit of a wait, so if I head back to our surgery then please will you give me a ring when Mrs Spencer is ready to drop home." explained Elly.

"Yes of course we will, thank you for bringing her in." replied the receptionist.

It took about an hour before the call came through.

"Hi Elly, it's Rachael from the health centre, Mrs Spencer's ready to go home."

Elly grabbed some scones and cream which had been bought in by one of the vet nurses for afternoon tea. "Mrs Spencer will love one of those, she can have my one." Elly said as she walked out of the door.

Having picked Mrs Spencer up, who fortunately only had bruising and a small cut to her arm, they arrived back at the farm.

"I have brought you some scones and cream for a treat as I am sure you will need a cup of tea soon." Elly smiled and popped the scones on the wall as she helped Mrs Spencer out of the car.

"Thank you dear, but before you go can we just check on the cow that is due to calve please?" Mrs Spencer just needed a hand to check on her cow and the shippen door was quite stiff she explained.

On opening the shippen barn door, Elly was surprised at what she saw.

"Oh dear, she is already giving birth." Mrs Spencer said.

Not only was the cow trying to give birth, she was also tied up with a chain to the metal rails inside and looked very uncomfortable.

"We need to untie her so that she can stretch out." Elly knew she had to act quickly.

Mrs Spencer was unable to help, but with a bit of a struggle and pulling Elly managed to free the Cow from her chain. She then got on her mobile to the surgery.

"It's Elly, I've just bought Mrs Spencer back from the

health centre and she wanted me to check a cow that's due to calve, and the cows calving now. Please can you get one of the vets here as soon as possible to help." Elly pleaded.

"I'm not sure we have anyone free, but I will try and let you know." said Jake who was the receptionist.

The cow was contracting, and there was a calf's leg appearing out of her. She was also tired, maybe due to struggling from being tied up, but maybe just due to the calving process.

"Can't you pull the calf off her Elly?" Mrs Spencer asked

"I will try the surgery again, they must have a vet here soon." Elly replied she had only ever helped sheep in lambing before, and also helped vets calve cows but never attempted one on her own.

"I will try the surgery again." Elly phoned the practice.

"Sorry Elly, we just don't have anyone free." Jake answered

"Ok, I will have a go, if I struggle then we will have to get a vet here and quick!"

With that Elly rolled up her sleeves. She knew that it was important to make sure that both legs were present, and that they were both forelegs and not hind legs. Mrs Spencer had found a bottle of lubrication and Elly emptied some around the legs of the calf inside the cow.

"I am sure you can do it Elly." Mrs Spencer gave Elly some words of support.

After about fifteen minutes, and some strong pulls to coincide with the cows own contractions, Elly managed to deliver the young calf. It was a male bull calf and quite large. Elly removed the afterbirth from the calf's nose and it drew in the air and gave a sneeze and shake of it's head. She drew a sigh of relief, and pulled the large calf towards the cows head so the mother could clean it off herself.

"Can we take them over to the barn I have ready?" asked Mrs Spencer who was delighted with alive calf.

Elly pulled a face, but wanted to please Mrs Spencer.

"It's too heavy to carry, do you have a sack that I could drag him on please?" Elly asked.

With that, Mrs Spencer went off to find a feed sack, and Elly rolled the calf onto it and started to pull the calf out of the shippen with the cow following. Mrs Spencer then decided to try and lift the other end of the sack and Elly could see the cow could knock the frail lady over again.

"It's OK, I will do it, you don't want to get knocked over again." Elly explained.

But Mrs Spencer insisted. Once in the barn, Elly said "Right lets leave them to it now", she could see that the cow was agitated and just wanted to be on her own with her new offspring. She didn't see what was coming next.

"Don't you tell me what to do on my farm!" shouted Mrs Spencer.

With that Elly left the barn and walked back to her car. Mrs Spencer followed.

"I'm sorry, thank you for calving the cow for me." said Mrs Spencer.

"No problem, just remember to rest your arm, and eat your scones." Elly replied she smiled and drove back to the surgery.

Once back at the surgery, Elly told the team what had happened. "I've calved a cow, it was traumatic, hard work but exciting." The team all thought she had done well.

"You have saved Mrs Spencer the cost of a visit charge and the cost of a calving fee and also probably saved the cow and calves life." smiled Jake.

Once the vets were back at the surgery they too praised Elly for her efforts. Elly was still chuffed that she could help not only Mrs Spencer but the cow too.

"I must ring Mrs Spencer's grandson who works at the dairy farm at Ivybridge, just to let him know that his grandma's been in an accident with the fall and may need a hand to feed the cows later." Elly felt sorry for Mrs Spencer.

"That's a good idea, she is stubborn, but at least if you warn him, she will get to rest her arm." said PK.

Elly phoned the farm where Mrs Spencer's grandson worked, and explained the story to the owner.

"Yes of course, we will get the message to him." replied Mr Phillips.

Elly thought nothing more of it and got on with the rest of her day, until she received a call from Mrs Spencer.

"Don't you interfere with my life, you busy body, how dare you phone my grandson!" Mrs Spencer shouted.

Elly was so shocked that she couldn't reply, and just hung up. So much for doing her good deed of the day. Not only providing a free taxi service to and from the health centre, providing scones and cream, calving a cow resulting in a live calf and cow at no cost to the farmer. There seems to be no pleasing some people. She was clearly upset, but the team at the surgery supported her.

Chapter Six

Elly was settling into her role at the branch practice in Modbury. She had a good team to manage, with Gail the receptionist who was like an auntie to her, along with Heather the theatre nurse who had been her student before qualifying, and then there was Jake, another part time receptionist come auxiliary, who was like a younger brother to her. Her job description suited her as not only to oversee the running of the branch, but also to assist with the radiography which took her off the beaten track and out of the surgery daily with the wide variety of cases she was asked to take images of. It also gave her time to give vital nursing care to Grace the foal, who both Elly and Lilly worked hard at getting her to stand without the use of splints which she was quickly outgrowing. The whole team was fond of Grace and were willing her to win the battle and get stronger.

The girls had been gradually removing the splints and applying physiotherapy in between. They would do this one limb at a time, and whilst the first had seemed to get stronger quicker, the right foreleg took longer.

After a few hours, Elly replaced the splint on Grace's leg.

"There babe, It may be a little sore, but I don't want you to stress out, you are confused as to why you can't walk without it." Elly stayed with Grace, and agreed with Lilly to change over at 5am.

Steve had arranged to visit in a couple of days, and hard as it was they all agreed that they would then make a decision on Grace.

Three days had passed, and the girls were again shattered. Their hard work was about to pay off, Grace had turned a corner, and could now get up on her own, with one splint on and the other leg with the sore, just bandaged.

"Well done girls, you have done an amazing job, but you now have to do the same with the other leg, I will come out again in another three days."

Many hours of intensive care followed, but seeing Grace get stronger and stronger was a reward which kept Elly and Lilly going.

By the time Grace was six weeks old, she could get up and down on her own with only light support bandages, and was again enjoying frolicking around with Minty in the stable.

When Grace was two months old, one of the national newspapers did a feature on her and Minty. Pictures were in the paper of them both curled up together and another of Grace stood walking around the yard with her support bandages on.

The support bandages were finally removed, Grace and Minty were turned out into a small paddock with Molly, who was an elderly hunter mare that was stabled next to Grace. She had been weaned onto milk pellets, as the scours and a painful bout of colic, meant that they could no longer keep her on the bottle. As Steve had explained there is always a risk with antibiotics in young foals, but the wound on her fetlock may not have healed without them.

All thoroughbred foals have to be microchipped and DNA tested for parentage. It was decided that Grace was strong enough to have this done, but it wasn't easy. The microchip has to be injected into their neck, and the blood test is also something which young foals dislike. Grace had already had more than her fair share of being prodded and poked. Ruth was a lovely young lady vet who volunteered for the job of microchipping and blood testing Grace. Elly thought that although Grace may fidget, neither of them were prepared for the strength that Grace showed when trying to avoid another needle. They literally had to rugby tackle her and pin her down.

"She is so strong now," said Ruth having dusted herself off from the straw she had rolled in whilst tackling the cheeky foal.

Elly and Lilly were unsure of the future for Grace. They wanted to see how she continued to grow. Lilly announced that she was pregnant, and maybe it was emotions from the pregnancy that had made her take on the enormous task of bringing up a premature orphan foal with Elly.

Elly took Grace to Steve's place. Steve had offered his paddocks free in return for some house sitting, which Elly jumped at. They found another thoroughbred youngster for Grace to mature with. Minty stayed with Molly at the yard. He was castrated, and kept as a pet sheep. Minty did try to escape the castration which was done at the surgery. One of the nurses didn't have a good hold of him properly as she wasn't expecting him to be naughty as he made a bold bid to escape, with several nurses and vets chasing after him. He was soon caught and the operation to castrate him went ahead.

Chapter Seven

The one thing that Elly loved about her job in the practice is that no two days were ever the same. With the variety of work and the location of the practice in the beautiful South Devon countryside it would attract vet staff from far and wide. One day she had a call from Mary, the practice manager at the Kingsbridge surgery.

"We have two young Irish men coming down for an interview, one we hope will work at the Ivybridge branch and one with you at Modbury, I wonder if you can ask the team there if they would like to join us for supper at the Start Bay Inn at Slapton." Mary asked.

"Yes what a great idea, and great location, I am sure the team will like that." Elly replied.

"Great, you will get to meet them in the afternoon beforehand anyway as we will show them around the surgeries." Mary explained.

"I will look forward to meeting them, I love the Irish accent." giggled Elly.

The team met the lads Dan and David when they were shown around the surgery for a guided tour. They both had a lovely bedside manner and looked ideal for a job within the surgery. With their Irish accents, Dan had a mesmerising southern Irish accent, whilst David was from Northern Ireland, and although his accent was sharper, his looks were dashing, and would be sure to draw in the horsey lady clients.

"Hi I'm Elly, and manage the branch here, along with my radiography skills which I use to back the horsey vets up with." she blushed.

"Nice to meet you." replied Dan he continued "I am more

skilled with the small animal side of things, whilst Dave is the one more interested in the horses."

"I am sure you will have a good time if taking the jobs, not only is the work varied with enough staff to support you, but we will also show you what this stunning area has to offer." Elly giggled.

The team were all treated to a fun night out at the Start Bay Inn which has a fantastic view of the long beach at Torcross. They got to meet the Irish lads in a more relaxed manner and were sure they put on a good impression to persuade them to take the jobs on offer.

Mary's plan had worked, Dan and David were employed and were to start their jobs in a couple of weeks time.

Elly received a phone call from Mary.

"The boys are starting work in a couple of weeks, and I thought of a great way to introduce them to the clients would be for them to judge at the Kingston Pet Show. What do you think Elly?"

"That's a good idea, there is a great local atmosphere, and the pet show is good fun. I will help them of course." replied Elly.

It was a tradition that every year the practice would supply judges for the Kingston Pet Show which was also part of their fun day. Elly phoned the secretary Fiona.

"Would it be OK if two of our new Irish Vets Dan and David are your judges at the pet show please?" asked Elly.

"That would be good, can you be their steward too?" asked Fiona.

"Yes I am happy to do that, and will take them in the beer tent afterwards, I am sure it will tempt them." replied Elly who was thinking of spending some quality time in the lads company.

Judging at pet shows is always tricky, especially if you are a new vet trying to make a good impression. There is always a knack of sharing out the prizes fairly, and not just to pot hunters looking for rosettes and prizes. This pet show was always a hoot and would provide good entertainment for the spectators too.

When Elly asked the lads if they would do it they were eager "Especially if there is a free pint or two, we would love to." replied Dan when asked.

Well the day didn't disappoint. Neither did the Irish lads. Elly enjoyed guiding them around the classes which ranged from usual best male and female dog, to rabbits and then most unusual pet which was won by a young lad who knew the care of how to look after his gecko. Dan and David had excellent bedside manner with both the adult owners and the kiddies and Elly knew they would be loved dearly by all the clients and animals in their care at the surgery. After the last class, they headed off to the bar and Elly was able to introduce the lads to some of the locals who were very welcoming.

"I think you have found a couple of gems there, who will be an asset to the practice" smiled Fiona who treated them all to a well earned drink at the bar.

"I didn't find them, but I am sure I'm going to look after them." giggled Elly.

Chapter Eight

Elly finally found her opportunity to study for the Equine Nursing certificate. The nursing team at the Royal College Of Veterinary Surgeons, together with Professor Tim Greet and the British Equine Veterinary Association had worked hard at finalising the course programme. A select few nurses had been signed onto the initial course and they had all passed. They were mainly from the larger Equine Hospitals. Elly was delighted to be registered onto the second term with a handful of other nurses.

The course was run as a block release, where the students would complete most of the study in their own practices completing case logs, whilst also attending an informative trip to Hartpury College in Gloucestershire, where they would study the theory side of the course. Elly's practice had supported her with the study in seeing as much practical cases as she could, whilst she self funded the fees. It was her dream to be qualified as an Equine Nurse, and get to look after many horses in her care. Although her practice did have a limited number of hospitalised cases, so in this instance Elly needed to find a work experience placement somewhere.

"How about you come to our hospital practice in Lambourn for a week Elly." offered Susan who was one of her fellow nurses at college.

"That sounds great, I love racehorses, it sounds an ideal location." Elly replied.

"We could do with some extra help, you would have to do night duties, but at the same time you will get the case logs which you need." Susan added "I will ask my boss Paul when I get back."

Elly's passion for racehorses had grown ever since she had joined her practice. She assisted one of the older vets Roy in analysing the blood samples which had been collected from racehorses at a local training yard in Hendham. The vets were under enormous pressure to get quick decisions if a horse needed to race but wasn't 100% in itself. The blood analysis would either reveal an infection normally in its lungs or if the horse is responding to a virus. This part of the job fascinated Elly. Then with the way her job was evolving into radiography and assisting Steve the Equine vet at the Modbury practice with his racecourse vetting duties, she was not going to turn down an opportunity to head to Lambourn for a week.

It wasn't long before the call came.

"Hi Elly it's Susan here, Paul is fine about you coming up. How about in two weeks time? We have a member of staff off on holiday and could do with some help. We can let you have a room in the house here which is at the bottom of Lambourn Down hill and has a great view of the gallops."

"That sounds ideal, I will check with my boss that I can have the week off, even if I take it as holiday, I am sure they won't mind." Elly explained.

Elly was excited about her trip to Lambourn. She had never been there before, and the thought of spending a week in a racing bias village sounded awesome. At the time the practice was mainly male vets with many female nurses and some good male ground staff who not only kept the upkeep of the surgery facilities in order but also helped with the young thoroughbred horses which were often a handful to treat.

As she drove through the village towards Upper Lambourn she could see the strings of horses which were heading up the hill for their daily exercise. Elly found all the riders to be courteous and they smiled and waved her passed as she drove slowly by them.

On her arrival at the hospital she was met by Susan. "I will show you around." Susan smiled.

Elly was shown to her accommodation which was a barn type chalet with a fabulous view from her bedroom window of the gallops on the hill. Susan then took her around the stables which were plenty, well built and full of sick or injured horses. There was a separate isolation box for the very sick. The hospital itself was well equipped, with a laboratory room, pharmacy, examination room, a knock down box for those horses needing surgery equipped with winches to transport the horses onto an operating table and a large very clean operating room. There were also a few offices for the staff too.

Susan introduced Elly to the team of vets she would be working with, Guy, Tony, Rupert and Billy. They were all welcoming. All the vets worked on a rota of inside hospital work and outside visits to the local racing yards. Susan also introduced Elly to Derek who was the main auxiliary who was in charge of the assisting team of ground staff.

"Hi Elly, do come and find me if you have any problems and need help with any of the hospitalised horses." he told her.

"Thank you, I will try not to bother you too much but I'm pleased to know you are there." replied Elly.

Elly had been allocated two nights on duty over the week, and was there to help and assist during the day which would also help her get some more case loads for her qualification.

Susan and Derek then headed off to help unload a weanling foal which had been brought in by one of the stud farms. Elly shadowed Guy the vet who was getting some medication ready for the foal.

"The foal has got a bad case of scours, runny diarrhoea which has left him dehydrated. He needs extensive fluid therapy and medication whilst we find out what has gone on at the stud farm to cause this."

Guy showed Elly where to find all the necessary medication, such as bags of fluid therapy which contained the correct essential electrolytes to maintain body function. He grabbed a five litre bag of Hartman's solution and placed in a microwave to warm to the correct temperature. Along with a tray full of essential items such as intravenous catheters together with a three way tap, giving sets, scissors, medicated povidine, surgical spirit, clippers and some soft bandage and vetrap. He added some blood sampling tubes and faecal bottles too, and a few pairs of gloves.

"We may have to do barrier nursing with this one Elly, so it is good you are here, the foal can be your case." Guy explained.

Chapter Nine

Elly rose to the challenge of nursing the foal which had been brought into the hospital in Lamborn with an enteric problem. She was pleased she had something to focus her week around, and although it meant she couldn't get hands on with any of the other inpatients due to the strict isolation rules, she still enjoyed her stay.

She would monitor the vital signs on the foal during the day and night, taking regular heart and respiratory rate and regular temperature checks. The weanling had been put on a multiple drip line so it was easy to transfer to the next drip bag of Hartmans without having to race off to the pharmacy at the practice to replace another bag. It was quite warm too, so no real need to heat bags up individually. Elly was also becoming fond of the youngster and enjoyed giving some real tender loving care which came naturally to her.

"You are getting fond of that young one, have you named him yet?" asked Guy the vet as he was peering over the door.

"Yes!" replied Elly "I am naming him Snufit, as he will not Snufit whilst on my watch!" she smiled.

"Doh he better had not." replied Guy.

Elly knew that the foal was sired by the famous stallion Sadler's Wells who she had followed his young stock with interest, and was also the sire of Grace her own youngster.

It was early days but the tests had come back from the laboratory and the young weanling had got *Lawsonia Intracellularis* which is a bacterial infection that gets into the small and sometimes large intestine. It often is an infection in pigs, but in this instance it is thought that it came over from a mare which was imported from a stud farm in America. It was no surprise that Snufit's paddock mate was also rushed into the hospital showing the same symptoms. At least the practice could treat accordingly and he could make a swift recovery. On the third day, Snufit had a relapse, he started to colic roll with pain. He had a new drug, which seem to be working fast, but did give him some gut pain. Elly went to the office to find some help. Guy was out on his visits, but she found the boss Paul in his office.

"Hello Paul, you need to come and see the weanling, he is starting to colic." Elly explained.

"What medication is he on?" Paul asked.

"They have put him on Erythromycin after his laboratory results came back." Elly informed him.

"Paul grunted, got off his seat and duly went to the medicine cabinet and drew up some medication."

Elly had trotted off behind him and held Snufit whilst he had his injection through his catheter in his neck.

"That should sort him. Stay with him and let me know if he doesn't get better within twenty minutes." Paul said as he walked away.

Elly monitored Snufits heart rate which had increased but started to settle. His respiratory rate was also returning to normal and he looked more comfortable. Guy appeared over the door. " That was a close one Elly, just as well you were with him."

"As I said, he won't Snufit on my watch." replied Elly.

Snufit continued to improve, much to Elly's relief. She enjoyed the rest of her stay at the hospital and although due to the strict hygiene regulations she couldn't help with the nursing of the other inpatients, she enjoyed the environment and was able to get some case logs done for her exam. Not only just with Snufit, but she also managed to help with practical laboratory work on two other cases that came in. One being a joint flush which was done under anaesthetic in the theatre which she could watch through a glass window. The other was a colic surgery which was not Snufit, but could also be viewed through the window and used as a case log.

Elly left the hospital at the end of the week. She would miss the team and Snufit, who was well on the road to recovery. She would keep in touch with Susan who was one of her classmates at college.

She was then able to follow Snufit's progress through his career as a young racehorse. He went into training as a three-year-old, and although never won a big race he had a couple of Group Three races to his C.V. He was then retired to stud early as the owners knew that he may not ever win one of the bigger races, but on breeding he was worth trying at stud. Before he headed off to stud Elly was lucky enough to visit him at the racing yard where he was in training. She was shown into his stable, and she thought that he recognised her as he bent his head down and gentle snuffled into her hand. Elly was thrilled she had the opportunity to see and touch him again. It meant the moon to her.

"He does recognise you, and he has been a joy to look after while he has been here." explained his young stable hand.

Chapter Ten

You never know, whilst working in a vet surgery who will walk through the door next. This day held a particular memory for Elly, when late one afternoon Susan rushed through the door.

"I think Amy has fallen off her horse? I found her walking the lanes in Kingston, she is wearing a riding hat and insists that she is just out walking the dogs." she continued, there are no dogs with her and definitely no horse, so I thought I would bring her straight in."

"OK thank you Susan, I will take a look." Elly was used to injured animals being rushed into the surgery, but not injured humans.

Elly went out to the car with Susan and found Amy sat in the passenger seat.

"What's happened to you?" Elly asked Amy.

"I was out walking the dogs, they ran off, and that's when this lady stopped, but she insisted I got in the car." Amy replied.

"Why are you wearing a riding hat?" Elly asked.

"I haven't got a hat on!" Amy shrieked.

Elly looked at Susan, and they both encouraged Amy out of the car.

"Are you able to sit with Amy please Susan? I will phone PK and call the doctors surgery too."

Elly phoned the doctors surgery. "If it's a head injury you must call an ambulance." they advised "And don't let her take her hat off."

The team had also managed to get hold of PK who was on his way back from the farm he was on which was some twenty minutes away.

"What has she done now?" he continued " I bet she has fallen off that damn horse Amigo, she must have been riding if wearing a hat."

Elly organised one of the young vets to go with one of the nurses to PK's house to firstly see if the dogs were there, and secondly to see if Amigo was there. They had tried to question Amy as to where the horse might be, but she insisted she hadn't been out riding.

"You go on the search Heather, if you go with Julie and keep in touch. Let us know if the dogs are at PK's house first as he will be worried." asked Elly.

It was about 5.30pm and Elly couldn't close the surgery until six, but assured Heather and Julie that she would join in on the search then.

PK arrived back just before the ambulance arrived. He was cross but kept his cool, as he could see Amy was confused. They managed to keep her hat on until the paramedics got there. Once they arrived the team of paramedics assessed Amy and decided to get her to hospital. Pk followed in his truck.

Heather and Julie had reported back that the dogs were in the house.

"Can you go on a hunt for Amigo please? He could be anywhere, and being black if he isn't found before dark could cause an accident, and even so could cause one anyway if loose on the road." Elly added "I will come and join the hunt at 6pm, as soon as I've shut here."

"Ok we will see you in a bit." replied Heather.

In the meantime Elly phoned many of the local farmers to see if they had any sight of a loose horse. Once 6pm arrived she headed off to join in the search.

But no sooner as she headed towards the area around PK's house she bumped into Heather and Julie coming the other way.

"Have you found him?" Elly asked.

"No" came the reply from Julie who went on to say "I think it's pointless, a bit like looking for a needle in a haystack."

Elly was cross, they had to find Amigo, he was a nervous horse and could be fully tacked up and scared and running loose on the roads. She knew it was a race against time.

"Heather, you jump in with me and let's keep looking." and with that Heather, without hesitation jumped in Elly's car and they continued the search for Amigo.

By this time several farmers and locals had heard about Amy's fall and joined in the search. They would use a base behind the shop car park at St Annes Chapel, and compare notes as to which area they had searched. Time was running out, it was 8pm and still no sign of him and it was starting to get misty with the sea fog heading in.

Then farmer Jack who was on his ATV arrived "I've just seen a horse in the field about half a mile away, it must be Amigo as he has his tack on, he is nervous and I can't get near him."

Elly jumped on the back off his ATV, whilst Heather took over driving and followed with Vicky one of the local horse ladies as company.

They arrived at the field, another farmer Eric was standing watching by the gate.

"I thought I would stay here just in case the horse took off." Eric explained.

"Thank you." replied Elly she was touched so many locals had turned up to help with the search, it proved how well respected both PK and Amy were in the area.

Elly and Vicky entered the field.

"Steady on." they whispered to Amigo who was spooked and covered in sweat.

One of the farmers had a bucket with some horse nuts in

it that he had stolen from his wives feed shed. They proved vital, as Vicky was able to tempt Amigo with a hand held full of nuts and the bucket as a bribe. Another farmer had brought some water, which again was a life saver. Amigo had been sweating and wouldn't have drunk for several hours. The team were able to remove his saddle and get him to take a drink of water.

"Now to get him home." Elly said.

Vicky was a very competent horse woman and insisted on leading Amigo. They left his bridle on for extra control and both Elly and Vicky walked Amigo the three mile journey back to his stable and safety. As it was getting dark, Heather drove Elly's car some distance behind them to avoid another potential accident, with Jack the farmer with his ATV lead they way with their lights on.

Elly was able to phone PK and give him the good news to pass to Amy that the dogs were fine and Amigo had been caught and looked not to be injured.

Vicky had been suffering from a bad back, but even so still insisted on helping Elly walk Amigo home. Elly was really grateful to Vicky, as Amigo was still very spooked and could have headed off again at any time.

By the time the girls and team made it back to the stable yard, PK had arrived home.

"They are keeping Amy overnight and want to re assess her in the morning, they may give her a head scan." PK was relieved but very concerned.

He was grateful to all in the team who sorted the recovery of Amigo. They all sat in the garden where PK opened a bottle of wine and offered all a celebration drink for their time and effort. Amy came home the following day having been given the 'all clear' by the doctors. PK banned her from riding Amigo for a month after.

Chapter Eleven

Something that Elly found about working in a mixed species vet practice is that she would never be bored with the work. Although her passion was horses, she was still keen to assist wherever needed. A perfect example of this was when she received a phone call from an elderly lady who was clearly stressed.

"Hello is that the vet practice?" the lady enquired.

"Yes, its Summerhill Vets, my name's Elly, how can I help?" Elly asked, she had already introduced herself when she answered the phone, but the lady had missed the intro.

"It's Mrs Butler here from Back Lane, you must come quick, there is a strange bird on my doorstep." the lady was clearly agitated.

"Can you describe the bird to me Mrs Butler please?" asked Elly.

"It's quite big, and just stood there. I tried to shoo it away but it wouldn't go. I think its injured as has blood running down its face."

"Can you take a picture of it for me and send it to us please Mrs Butler." Elly was hoping that maybe they could identify the size of the bird to identify it and see what size carrier they would need to take.

"I can't do that my dear, I have no idea how to take pictures and send them on my mobile." She added you need to come quick, I think it is an exotic bird."

"Don't worry Mrs Butler, I will get someone to you as soon as possible." Elly tried to reassure Mrs Butler.

The only vet Elly had at the surgery at that moment in time was Steve her boss.

"I've had a call from Mrs Butler who says she has an exotic bird landed on her doorstep and wants us to go and fetch it." Elly found Steve in his office just about to take a sip of his cup of tea.

Almost spitting his tea out Steve reacted "You are kidding me?"

"No she is serious." replied Elly trying to keep a straight face and continued "You are the only vet here so someone needs to go."

Steve looked at her questioningly, and realising Elly was being serious he said "OK, Ok I will go, but you will have to come with me. We will need to take a cage and protective gloves if you can get them ready please Elly?"

Elly grinned and hoofed it down the stairs to get the equipment ready. Steve shouted down the stairs "Oh and load up the dog catcher wire too, we may need to run around her garden after it."

Elly could hear Steve muttering to himself and she giggled as she told Gail the receptionist where they were off to.

"You go careful, we want you all coming back in one piece." Gail said as they left the surgery.

This was another instance where the team would go to help a stricken animal and not be paid for it, it was another for the health and welfare of the animal and the stressed old lady who couldn't leave her house to go out as an exotic bird was manning her doorway.

"I wonder what bird it will be?" Elly was guessing as they approached the edge of Mrs Butler's garden.

"I bet it's a pheasant." said Steve who continued "It's the end of the shooting season, it may have an injured wing."

When they arrived at the door equipped with protective gloves, cage and wire dog catcher, they could identify the bird immediately.

"It's a Cockerel, there will be no need for the equipment

47

other than the cage to put it in." Steve said laughingly to Elly

They could see Mrs Butler looking through the window obviously scared out of her life.

Steve picked up the cockerel and had a brief look at its face.

"Looks like he has been in a fight and had his eye pecked at. I'm guessing he lost the fight and ran here for safety." Steve suggested.

He placed the cockerel in the cage and passed it to Elly. "You put him in the car please whilst I have a chat with Mrs Butler."

Steve explained to Mrs Butler that it was only a cockerel and nothing exotic. He also explained to her that they would take it back to the surgery and treat it, then try and find it's owner.

"I am very grateful, thank you for taking it from my doorstep, I was quite afraid." replied Mrs Butler.

"No problem my dear, you take care." came his reply.

Back at the surgery they were able to clean up the cockerel and treat him for shock. They left him in a quiet dark room and Elly set about trying to locate his owners. This wasn't easy, they thought he would be locally owned but nobody came forward. They kept him in overnight and the following day he looked much brighter, although looked to have lost his sight in one eye.

"I'm going to call him Nelson." Elly smiled when she told Gail.

Fortunately one of the farmers they phoned had offered to take Nelson, if his owner couldn't be located which ended up being the case. He was placed in with some lovely hens to his delight and lived a few years in happiness with his brood.

They will never know the full story of how he found his way to Mrs Butler's doorstep, but were very pleased with the outcome.

Chapter Twelve

A call came from one of Elly's friends, Anne, about accompanying her on a trip to Hungary, where her daughter Rosy was competing with her Welsh Section D pony stallion Bailey, in the European driving event.

"Hi Elly, we need a vet nurse to travel over to Hungary with us, we are going for a week at the end of the month to compete in the English team going there, would you like to come along please?"

Anne knew that Elly had been to Hungary before to try and locate her family ancestry, and the trip could work for both of them.

"I'd love to Anne, thank you for asking me, as long as I can get a week off work I can go."

Elly checked with her boss Steve.

"That sounds an ideal way of doing some more case logs for your certificate Elly, yes of course you can have that week off." he replied.

The practice had to do some vital blood work on Bailey before he could go. He was tested for general haematology, liver and kidney function and tapeworm assay. He also had to be vaccinated against West Nile Virus before travelling. All this in preparation for the trip made it more exciting for Elly. She had travelled to Budapest once before with a friend who showed her around the city, and also the music school where her relative who she was trying to trace went to school. Maybe she would get another chance to follow up on her previous visit which had proved negative.

It was August, and she knew it would be hot. Medications which she could take with her were limited due to the transport lorries already being overloaded. There was no vet travelling with the team, as they had been told that a list of veterinarians were available throughout the countries in which they travelled through. Also vets were based at the competition yard once they got there. One of the competitors uncles was to travel with the team, he was a retired cattle vet from Wales, and could also administer first aid if needed.

Elly consulted with the vets at her surgery to agree what she could take along.

"They all carry their own electrolytes, so maybe I should take a thermometer, a stethoscope, intrasite gel, melonin dressing, soffban, a few vetrap bandages some scissors and artery forceps." Elly inquired.

"That sounds ideal Elly, it covers first aid and the team will have extra bandages for travelling anyway." said Steve who added "Hopefully the Welsh vet should have some pain relief with him."

The team all met up at Dover where they had to camp overnight, before heading off at 5am the following morning. Elly had also been asked to share the driving of one of the owners BMW complete with caravan and the ladies two teenage sons. She had never driven abroad before, especially not towing a caravan, but had travelled to France with her ex-husband so was aware of navigating around the complicated European roads. She agreed to do this too.

They started off in convoy with the lorries carrying the horses. They were heading to Frankfurt Racecourse which was their first night stopover. The picturesque journey took twelve hours. They had short stops enroute, and with two drivers they were able to rest on a shift basis. Elly found it easier to drive on the autoroutes and hugged the metal barriers on her right shoulder. They made it in good time.

Once in Frankfurt they struggled to find their way into the racecourse, going around the city a couple of times, before flagging down some very cute police officers who then convoyed them in. The temperature at 7pm was reaching 32 degrees and they knew that the horses would need rehydrating once there. To their horror they found that the allocated boxes did not have half stable doors but were huge metal doors with no openings to fresh air.

"We need to sort some half doors before the horses get here." Anne was concerned as everyone else was.

The team of about fourteen parents and helpers made a huge effort to compromise makeshift barriers for the stable doors. They had a bit of help from the Frankfurt race team, who guided them to available barriers to use. They were not allowed to move the horses into the better stable accommodation due to quarantine laws. Once the horses arrived they were put safe in their makeshift airy stables and the team got together for a picnic supper.

On the second day they again rose at 5am to get on the road before the heat set in. They had already travelled 400 miles and had another 680 miles to their destination. The huge transporter lorries for the horses were well equipped with air conditioning.

The road down through Germany and then Austria were beautiful. So many mature lush pinetree lined autoroutes. The journey through the tyrolian villages through western Austria were stunning. At around 4pm the crossed the border into Hungary. One of the drivers had a scare as she thought she had lost her driving licence but found it inside her passport. She had fun really trying to communicate with the border patrol who were quite sweet.

Once negotiating the autoroute around Budapest, they managed to locate the competition ground. The text were flying as people were getting lost, but by 8pm all had arrived including the horses.

One horse suffered a bad journey, a small mare named

Flicka had become tired and dehydrated. She staggered off the lorry. Elly checked her heart rate which was 50, with the normal being up to around 36. Flicka's respiratory rate had also increased to 25, and her temperature was raised at 39.5 degrees Celsius. She was in urgent need of fluids. The lorry driver admitted that she was the ones reluctant to drink water when he made his frequent stops.

The team acted fast and Elly dosed Flicka with some electrolytes via a dosing syringe. Her owner had bought some nourishing electrolytes with her. They also sponged the mare down with warm water gently to help her recover. Once in the stable Flicka soon started to settle. The team were all tired, but looking after the mare was important. The chef d'equipe and Elly kept monitoring the mare and once she had settled to normal vital signs of heart, respiratory rate and her temperature had dropped they took her out for a bit of lush grass which was on offer. They also decided on a rota overnight so that she was kept an eye on at all times.

After a two days rest, the team were working their ponies ready for the competition. They had a day to work them up, before having them all vet checked. At first Flicka's owner was going to withdraw her, but to their amazement she passed the vet check, so they would take it easy with her and see how she went. There was plenty of shade around the arena area to keep the ponies cool and lots of water on hand.

Elly placed herself by the water tap under the shade. She was able to watch the event going on in the arena, and had Timothy the lorry driver there for company. He had also volunteered to be a bucket holder if one of the team's ponies needed a drink. Elly was getting to know Timothy well, and enjoyed his company.

The temperature in the sun had reached 30 degrees again and it was only 10am. It was going to be a real hot day. Fortunately the team had been sensible listening to their elders and did not do too much of a warm up before entering the arena. Always offering them water and electrolytes when they rested.

The Hungarians were lying first in the 14 years and older dressage class, with the Austrians lying second, followed by the French and German teams. It was Bailey and Rosanna's turn next. Anne settled in the back of the trap, and the combination looked special. With the beautiful black stallion Bailey showing off his full presence, and Rossana guiding through the discipline with ease. The combination deservedly claimed second place off the Austrians, with the Hungarians in first. A huge cheer went up from the crowd from the English team. Even young Flicka and her driver William displayed a lovely dressage round and gained sixth out of twenty in the 12 to 14 year driver class. There was much celebrating to be had after the team had settled the ponies back in their stables.

Chapter Thirteen

Every evening after the day's driving event, the team and helpers were treated to an awards ceremony with plenty of Hungarian entertainment, which they all found amusing. Rosanna collected her award and the team all applauded her. They partied on until late, sampling the delights of Hungarian traditional hospitality. There were lots of speeches that seemed to go on forever being in seven different languages, and the youngster got through it giggling. They were watching the older members of the support group getting merry on Tokai, which was a potent Hungarian liqueur.

One of the grooms had been back to the stable block to check on the horses. It was just as well she did. It would seem that the naughty Hungarian travellers had offered their mares up to the stables where the ponies were and let them in to have a free service by one of the beautiful German stallions. "That is so naughty." she said to the lads as they quickly removed the mare from the stable and she rushed back to the party.

"You must come quick, there are some lads out there who have just led a mare into one of the boxes to get her served by a stallion for free. They may have another and have their eye on Bailey." Dawn sounded worried.

"That's sneaky." replied Anne as a group headed off out to check on their horses in the stable.

By this time the commotion had died down with many going to check that their ponies were safe.

Bailey was happy in his stable munching some hay.

"We will need to do night watch." explained Sarah the chef d'equipe.

"I am happy to do a shift." replied Elly.

"I am too." came the reply from Timothy.

Another offer came from George, one of the parents. And they all knew how important it was to keep an eye on all their ponies and not just Bailey, although he was the only entire stallion among the English team.

Elly was happy to do the early shift as she thought she would sleep well afterwards. Fortunately she had only had one liqueur and no wine, which had given her some courage to keep an eye on the stables without being drunk.

The night watch went without a hitch and all were ready to tackle the marathon stage of the event. Chef d'equip Sarah had worked hard to supervise that all the competitors were ready and on time for their classes. Overnight rain had softened the ground slightly which had been a worry, but the warm up areas had not been watered. The main ring itself had, which at least was some relief for the horses having to go fast against the clock.

Bailey again sparkled, in the event. He ran second in the marathon, having only got tight to one of the markers, which Rosanna was able to correct his position with only seconds lost. Elly again waited at the tap with her bucket of water and wet sponge. The temperature had dropped to 28 degrees which was more comfortable for both ponies and drivers. Bailey finished in a fast time to hold onto second place. However he had lost a shoe, which was a special shoe which he had built into his hoof with plastic. Not only did they need to find the shoe to replace it, but also to get it fitted back on his hoof.

The course was quiet long and went through various fields and terrain. The ponies had also had to gallop through a water lake, which is where Bailey could have lost his shoe.

Elly immediately went on the search for the missing shoe with Timothy. Bailey had been taken back gently to the stable area with Elly and Timothy agreeing to keep in touch via text.They headed off down the track and followed the route which was laid out as the course. The event was still going on, so Elly had to practice her pigeon Hungarian on the stewards to let them know why they were walking around looking on the track.

"Look Timothy, we are almost at the water pond feature, lets ask the steward if we can have a look for the shoe?"

"Good luck with that one Elly, your Hungarian is one hundred times better than mine, so you ask."

Elly giggled and approached the steward.

"Kérem, keresse meg a póni cipőt?" Elly asked, which in English is "Please can we look for the ponies shoe."

"Igen, de ne légy hosszú." came the reply from the steward which translated means "Yes but don't be long."

"Köszönöm." replied Elly which is thank you in English.

Timothy smiled. "I am well impressed Elly." when she explained to him what she had asked.

They both walked through the water pond at a distance of a meter apart to see if they could feel or walk on the shoe.

"This is tricky, It's like looking for a needle in a haystack!" Timothy encouraged Elly to come out of the water before the next competitor arrived. The stewards had whistled to them a warning.

"Maybe it was just loosened and he lost it on the home straight." Elly said hoping.

They were getting worried that the shoe couldn't be found, and that Bailey would not be able to continue on the final day of the competition. Elly was not prepared to give up in a hurry, and with the permission of stewards they searched around more obstacles but with no luck.

"Maybe it flicked off the course as he was turning?" Elly searched further away from the obstacles and then caught a glimpse of the shoe.

"There it is!" she squealed with delight and pick up the shoe.

"It's a bit bent, hopefully the farrier can correct it and get it stuck back on." Timothy pulled a face at the metal object Elly was holding.

They headed straight back to the stable block and passed over the bent shoe. "We have found a farrier, and I bought some glue along, just in case this happened. Well done you two for locating it." Anne was thrilled they had found the shoe.

That was the good news for the day, the bad news was unfortunately Flicka, who had suffered some exhaustion on the trip over had now damaged her tendon and gone lame during the marathon. The vet team on site were able to give first aid and inject Flicka with pain relief, also providing her with a large robert jones bandage to support her to get back to the stables. The bandage needed changing once the event had finished for the day so that the vet could examine it properly. The competition vet was a young Hungarian lady called Dora, who spoke good English.

"We need to replace the bandage every twelve hours and place an icepack on for ten minutes in-between." Dora explained.

"No problem, I can do that." replied Elly who was pleased to be able to demonstrate her equine nursing skills and give support relief to the pony.

The farrier was able to replace the shoe on Bailey, and they all hoped it would stay on for him to complete the event. The following day was a rest day, and it had been arranged as a treat for Elly that she would show some of the fathers who had gone on the trip to support their children, that she would show them around Budapest city. She had at least earned the time to be able to go back into the city to try and trace her family roots at the music school.

The following day Elly headed off with four of the fathers and Timothy for a trip to the city. They were well impressed with her skills at showing them around. Elly had been treated to a trip there the previous year by a friend who combined it with a business trip. They had stayed in a hotel alongside the river Danube on the Pest side which had a glorious market square. They stopped in a cafe for lunch and the chaps were also impressed that the waiters recognised Elly.

"I feel like a local and at home." Elly smiled.

They planned to call into the music school on their way home, which they did, however to Elly's horror it was closed for school holidays.

"I didn't plan for that!" Elly was disappointed that she couldn't again access the school and look through the year books in the library, which she had been allowed to do before.

"Oh well, it means I will have to come back again." she explained to the chaps, and they took her off to another cafe for a glass of wine to thank her for her guided tour.

The final day of the competition came. Bailey once again excelled himself and completed an excellent round of cones. He had two in hand, but would he be quick enough and would his shoe stay on?

The whole team watches around the edge of the arena. Bailey could not be warmed up much due his shoe problem. Once in the ring he flew around in a fast time and only hit one cone. The crowd again burst into applause and the team whistled to his victory. It had been a nail biting time, but he and Rosanna had kept their cool and were awarded bronze.

There were great celebrations to be had on the final evening with the award ceremony. With the team heading back on the long trip the following day. Elly was able to spend some quality time with Tim in his truck that night, but he had a girlfriend at home waiting for his return, which Elly knew about and respected.Flicka also made the trip home, with frequent bandage changes and syringe doses of pain relief which were supplied by the vet team at the event.

Chapter Fourteen

Elly loved her two black Labradors Bumble and Eryn. Bumble she had bred from her foundation bitch Echo, which she had the opportunity to use a local working dog to breed her with. Bumble had been sold to a young gardener chap to bring up with two boys. However when he split with his wife, David offered Bumble back to Elly for nothing.

"She is a lovely bitch, and I am sure you will look after her. Unfortunately now I have split from my wife, I am out working long days and in the summer its too hot for her to sit in the car." David explained.

"That would be lovely, as you know I only have Eryn now, who is half related to Bumble. I lost Echo with a tumour last year." Elly was thrilled to have the opportunity to have Bumble back.

Bumble had been spayed only three weeks before, as David didn't think he could cope with having her in season again.

"It is a shame you had her spayed, as you know I like the opportunity to keep the breeding line going." she added "But I will love her just the same."

David was pleased that Elly would take Bumble back on, he knew she would be looked after, and if he did want to see her he knew he could.

"The boys may want to take her out for an occasional walk if that's OK please Elly?"

"Yes of course, no problem, we can see how she settles in first." Elly wanted what was best for the family, as David's boys had started to grow up with Bumble who was only two.

All went well to start with. Bumble was quite a character

and apart from the episode when she had gone off into the barley fields with Bea whilst Elly was house sitting she had behaved impeccably.

After about six weeks, David phoned Elly to ask if his ex wife and sons could take Bumble for a walk to Bigbury Bay. It was towards the end of the school holidays and the boys were missing Bumble.

"That's fine, if Karen could pick her up from the Modbury surgery where I will be working in the morning." Elly asked

Bumble was pleased to see Jack, Robin and Karen.

"We have missed her, but I am working and the boys have lots of sports which they are into now, so it's good you have taken her back." Karen smiled and made a fuss of Bumble.

Bumble jumped into the car and headed off for her beach walk to Bigbury Bay. It was a hot summer day and Elly knew she would love a swim. She was also keen to keep the boys happy as she knew all too well how being brought up in a broken family can affect your childhood.

Only an hour had passed and a call came from the main surgery in Kingsbridge.

"Hi Elly its Lucy here one of the vets in Kingsbridge." she continued "We have had Bumble brought in by Karen who used to own her, she said they were out walking on the cliff path and saw Bumble bitten by a snake, she thought it may be an Adder."

"Oh my." replied Elly who realised how serious it could be.

"Well I understand that Bumble is now yours again, so we just need permission to give her an injection of cortizone?" Lucy explained that Bumble wasn't showing any signs of shock, but they could jab her and keep her in the surgery to monitor her condition.

"Yes of course, do whatever is necessary." Elly knew she was in good hands.

"OK Elly, we will jab her and keep an eye on her and keep you posted." Lucy was happy Bumble's Adder bite would hopefully respond to the injection.

It wasn't long before another call came from the main branch surgery, which had been closer to the beach.

"Hi Elly, it's Lucy again. I am afraid Bumble looks to be having problems breathing, her bite was on her neck which is now swollen, we need to get to the hospital in Kingsbridge to obtain some Viper antivenom. Are you OK with that? She added.

"There is always a risk with Viper Antivenom, but I think it's her best chance. She will be on a drip too." Lucy explained

Elly knew that Bumble was in good hands and trusted the vets at Kingsbridge. She also didn't blame Karen, and knew that Karen's quick response in getting Bumble to the surgery would hopefully save her life. How awful for the boy's Elly thought.

Lucy had sent a runner to the hospital which had reserved a dose of Viper Antivenom for them to collect. The area was becoming a known spot for Adders, although there had only been one or two dogs bitten over a few years. It was lucky the Hospital had a spare dose of Antivenom. Bumble was a natural working dog who loved flushing out pheasants, she had obviously been attracted by the movement and stuck her nose into somewhere she shouldn't have.

A call came from the surgery another hour later.

"Hi Elly, we have given Bumble the dose of Antivenom and she is responding well to that and the fluids she is on. Can you collect her after work from here and keep an eye on her overnight?" Lucy asked.

Elly was delighted "No problem, I will pick her up then, and thank you so much, I owe you!" she was well relieved that Bumble had responded, and even though she had insured Bumble, she would still look after Lucy and team for the care they had given her.

Elly also phoned Karen to let her and the boys know all was well. "Don't you worry at all, it could have happened at any time, well done for noticing the Adder else we may never have known what had bitten her or got the Antivenom in time." Elly explained.

As time went by all the branches held a dose of Antivenom in the surgery fridge. The hospitals could no longer let go of their stock as they needed it for humans. It had to be imported from Croatia at that time and retailed at only about £100 per dose. This has since gone up a lot in price to five times that. Bumble was a fortunate dog to get her dose administered quickly thanks to the quick thinking of the vet team on hand.

Chapter Fifteen

Having returned from a successful trip to Hungary with the driving ponies, Elly was keen to spend more time with her own bred ponies. Her youngster Enya had been given time to mature. Elly had broken her in herself, but for further schooling she sent the quirky young mare to a lady called Alex, who had a successful livery and training yard. The place had excellent facilities, with an indoor and outdoor school along with a proper showjumping course.

"She is quirky, can be very grumpy, but has shown us some real talent." explained Alex.

"It is just a shame I have no children of my own to ride her, but I am sure I will find a brave young soldier to ride her." replied Elly.

And that is what happened. Elly found a young teenager who could ride in juniors and was brave enough to give Enya the positive ride she needed. There had been plenty of offers, but knowing how quirky Enya could be, Elly had to be fussy. Kayley had been riding for many years throughout her childhood, she had lots of success in the junior showjumping circuit. To Elly, Kayley seemed an ideal character as she had quite a feisty manor too, so they appeared to be well suited. Judith the pony club tutor was a bit apprehensive when Kayley and Enya went for a schooling lesson.

"Enya's not going to be ready to affiliate for about another six months." was Judith's opinion.

"Well we see about that." Elly explained to Kayley when letting her know she had entered them for their first affiliated competition at Devon County Show in May.

"Oh that sounds ideal, we have a month to work on her."

Kayley was delighted.

Although they had taken on board what Judith had said regarding her concerns about Enya not being ready. Elly had taken things really slow with Enya and she was now six years old. She appeared to be talented and that is what they needed to prove. They schooled her over the next few weeks, and the week before Devon County they took her back to Alex's yard to get an opinion from Alex. Having popped her around a rather varied course of 90cm, which she flew around, Alex's face was a picture.

"Gosh, she has come on really well, you may as well take her along as you need to know how good she is." Alex remarked.

Elly and Kayley came away from Alex's with some hope in their heart that maybe Enya was ready to affiliate. There was a local indoor event the weekend before the County show which they took Enya along to. Admittedly it was only 70cm, but good to see how Enya and Kayley got on under pressure.

The show at Redpost was well supported, and Kayley had competed there often. She schooled Enya in the warm up arena and had no problem in getting a clear round.

"She felt amazing, really buzzed up and loved it." Kayley chirped.

There were twelve in the jump off and Enya was last to go. They entered the arena and Elly was really proud of her pony competing. It was such a shame that she hadn't any children of her own, as she would have been even prouder. Being black and Welsh cross Arab Enya looked a picture in the ring, with many commenting how stunning she looked.

The bell went and Kayley steered Enya gently into the first fence. Then she took off, it was as if she had wings. She flew around the course in the fastest time, but just rolled the last pole, and ended up fifth.

"Well done Kayley, you rode her really well." Elly thanked

Kayley.

"She was amazing, I can't wait until next week." Kayley beamed.

It had rained heavily two days before Devon County, and thoughts were that it might be cancelled. It went ahead and Elly drove Kayley and Enya up in the trailer. They had a natter on the way up.

"I just want you both to enjoy it. There is no pressure, just see how she goes. It may be slippery so take it steady." Elly didn't want either to come to any grief.

They walked the course together. The jumps seemed huge, but they were only 90cm, although it was as big as anything Enya had tackled. They agreed to only gently warm up Enya so that she didn't boil over. They both wanted to prove the riding club coach that Enya was ready to compete at that level.

There were thirty in the class and Enya's turn was next.

"Just remember to enjoy it." instructed Elly as Kayley and Enya trotted into the arena.

The bell went. The ground was very wet and slippery. Elly was biting her nails as she watch Charlotte and Enya approach the first fence, which was a standard uprite.

"Oh no she is gonna stop!" Elly spoke to Maggie, Kayley's mother, who had come to watch.

And with that Kayley managed to encourage Enya over the fence. Enya had just seemed to spook a little. Kayley then picked up the pace and Enya jumped around clear.

"Phew that was close!" Elly said to Kayley as they came out of the arena.

"I was just trying to go steady and she spooked." laughed Kayley relieved.

"Well done you are in the jump off, there are only five so far." Elly said as she offered Enya a well deserved polo and a good pat.

Kayley gently walked Enya around the warm up arena having given her ten minutes of rest and a well earned drink of water. She then memorised the jump off course with Elly. Once again Elly gave Kayley instructions just to enjoy the competition and to both come back safely in the slippery wet conditions. Enya was second to go in the jump off, which there were now nine clears.

The commentator announced their entry .

"Here now is Eastleigh Enya and Kayley Maddocks."

The bell went and off they flew, Kayley wasn't going to have another repeat of a near stop at the first fence. Elly felt really proud of the pony she had bred, now competing at County level. Once again they went clear in a fast time.

"Clear in a time of 39.5 seconds, Eastleigh Enya and Kayley Maddocks." he announced.

They then waited as one after the other the remainder of the clear rounds tried to beat their time, and once the last pony had gone and knocked a fence they knew Enya and Kayley had won.

"Well done, you were great." Elly cried as she praised Kayley and patted Enya, providing her with more polos and loosened her girth.

Maggie, Kayley's mother, had filmed the whole event, and they did a beautiful lap of honour. Enya being black and part Arab looked stunning in the victory lap around the arena. Elly was so proud.

Chapter Sixteen

Elly enjoyed life at the practice. She had a unique job, one that had evolved due to her showing a keen interest in Radiography. Her bosses had let her study for her Equine Nursing certificate, whilst managing the branch surgery and she would be allowed to assist the equine vets whilst completing her case logs. This took her off the beaten tack and travelling around the beautiful South Hams countryside. Not long after her Hungary trip, she was able to meet up with the lovely Bailey, the driving pony who had achieved Bronze place in the championship. Bailey had lost a shoe whilst competing, and this was no ordinary shoe, but had been purposely built for him. His farrier Derek had built the shoe especially to adapt to Baileys hoof, which had been previously damaged.

"Elly can you go and take x-rays of Baileys hoof please?" asked Steve her boss who added "As you know Bailey lost a shoe whilst competing and although the farriers at the event managed to replace it there, we now need to know how his foot balance is so Derek the farrier can re shoe him."

"Yes of course." replied Elly.

"Great, the farrier Derek has arranged to go along at 2pm and will look at the radiographs whilst you are there." Steve explained.

It was a very sunny day, and Elly loaded the works estate car ready for the visit. She knew Anne, the owners yard, would have some shady trees around the stable area. It can sometimes be difficult when looking at radiographs on a laptop on a bright sunny day, so using the estate car was quite useful in providing a dark environment inside to view them. She checked she had loaded all the equipment, x-ray generator, developer, extension leads, lead gowns for protection, gloves, markers, x-rite tape, metal holders and foot blocks for Bailey to stand on and all more importantly the x-ray digital plates which contained the film for the pictures. Elly also had to take warning signs for health and safety which had to be displayed around the area she would be working in to protect and warn any onlookers. Wearing lead gowns on a hot sunny day was far from flattering, can be heavy and cumbersome to work in, but were vital for body protection against any scatter from the x-rays. She also loaded a couple of thyroid protection neck covers too.

Elly knew many of the local farriers, as she would be often called out to x-ray many ponies and horses which needed farrier assistance. The most regular ones were laminitic ponies who needed special remedial farriery, or those just for trimming and foot balance. However she had never met Derek before that day at Anne's. Elly normally gets on well with the farriers and has some cheeky banter with them, but on this occasion she becomes a gibbering wreck. Derek looked like somebody out of a fit country and western modelling movie. He was tall, blonde and very fit, wearing jeans with a leather belt and chaps, along with a tight T Shirt which displayed his fit six pack. He also had a bit of rough but short designer stubble. Oh my days! Thought Elly.

"Hi Elly, meet Derek." Anne said as she introduced them.

"Hello Elly, nice to meet you." Derek smiled as Elly melted

"Nice to meet you too Derek." Elly giggled and blushed. I need to concentrate on the job Elly thought as she turned to unpack the x-ray generator out of the car. She looked at Anne, and Anne immediately knew what Elly thought of Derek. Anne giggled too.

Elly set up the equipment as quickly as she could. She placed a gown and thyroid cover on Anne who would be holding Bailey, and then dressed into the unflattering x-ray gown herself. She was pleased to see Bailey again after his triumph winning bronze in Hungary. Placing his hoof on the wooden block, she was able to place the x-ray plate behind in the slot and the first image was taken.

"That looked quick and easy." Derek said as he was watching from a safe distance." He then followed Elly to the back of the car where she placed the plate in the developer.

"Here is the first picture." Elly invited Derek to take a look at the image of Baileys foot which she had on the laptop screen in the back of the car.

"Can we zoom in on it a bit please Elly" asked Derek.

And with that Elly also leant in the car to zoom in on the picture. She found herself for a lush moment alongside Dan in the car looking at the image on the screen. He looked at her and for a moment she couldn't help but stare into his stunning blue eyes. Again she blushed, then moved out quickly embarrassed. Derek smiled Oh my days She thought and went back to Bailey with another plate.

"OK so we have the lateral view, shall I do the DP (Front) view now Derek?" Elly asked.

"Yes that would be fine thanks?" Dan again smiled as Elly melted, she was getting quite warm in the lead gown by now.

Elly went back over to where Anne was holding Bailey.

"He's nice isn't he?" Anne asked Elly knowing she was smitten.

"Yes he is lovely, where did you find him? I haven't seen him before" whispered Elly.

"He is ex military, now set up near Buckfastleigh, you will probably get to see him more." explained Anne.

"Gosh I do hope so." grinned Elly.

She took another image of Baileys hoof and again had another moment in the boot of the car whilst showing Derek the image.

Packing the equipment in the back of the car, Elly thanked Anne for holding Bailey and the girls took off their heavy x-ray gowns. Elly was pleased to be able to say goodbye to Derek without wearing the unflattering piece of clothing.

"Lovely to meet you Elly, I am sure we will see each other again." Derek went back to replacing the special shoe on Baileys hoof.

Once back at the surgery Elly told Gail the receptionist of her encounter with the lovely Derek.

"Gosh Elly you are naughty, I wondered why you came back grinning." said Gail.

"He was lovely, I couldn't help but melt." Elly laughed with Gail.

Derek had taken the surgery number just in case he had any queries about the radiographs of Bailey.

The following day Gail took the call from Derek.

"Elly it's Derek on the phone for you, looks like you made an impression." Gail giggled as she passed the call onto Elly.

"Hi Elly it's Derek, please may I have a copy disc of Bailey's x-rays, I would like to keep an eye on his progress." Derek explained, and added Oh and can I take you for a drink please?"

"Yes of course on both accounts." smiled Elly she continued "There is a party at the White Hart pub on Friday evening, would you like to come along?"

"That would be nice, I can pick up the x-ray disc then if you like?" Derek replied.

"Told you that you had made an impression Elly!" laughed Gail.

"Oh my days, I've got a date with the hunky farrier!" Elly danced around the surgery.

It didn't take long until the evening arrived. Gail had teased Elly all day, as she knew how keen Elly was. Elly was preoccupied with wondering what to wear, something tidy but not tarty she thought.

Elly had remembered to print off the x-ray images on disc for Derek. They had arranged to meet in the bar of the White Hart. Elly was nervous, but also keen with excitement. She knew little about Derek, whether he was single or attached, or even married, but was prepared to find out.

Derek arrived and after they enjoyed a drink in the bar, Elly took Derek up to the party which was happening in the function room above the pub. It was one of her friends Michele's 30th birthday party.

"Oh wow, where did you find him?" asked Michele who was also taken back by Derek's rugged but model-like appearance.

"We are just having a drink. I found him whilst at work." explained Elly.

"I'm gonna buy a horse quickly and he can be my farrier!" laughed Michele.

Elly was aware that most of the females at the party were staring at Derek. He seemed to take it in his stride and was obviously used to girls throwing themselves at him.

They left the party and he called into Elly's for a drink before heading home. They then had a kiss and a cuddle before he left. Unfortunately for Elly, Derek had been in the middle of a break up and was hoping to get back with his girlfriend. He was just looking for company at that stage which Elly gave him.

Chapter Seventeen

Knowing how disappointed that Elly would be that the date with Duncan didn't go quite as she would have hoped, Steve, her boss invited her to accompany him at the races. He was to be duty vet at Newton Abbot races and had to be part of a team looking after any horse that may have incurred an injury there.

"How would you like to come and assist me at the races Elly? It will be down the home straight, in-between around the track too?" Steve asked.

"That would be great, thank you?" Elly replied as she knew it could potentially help in her case logs for her Equine nursing too.

"You will have a bit of free time too Elly, I know that you are interested in racing and have lots of friends who will be there." Steve knew that Elly was fond of National Hunt racing, and she liked to follow the horses, especially those which she has had a chance to analyse the blood samples for too and watch their progression, also the youngsters progressing in their careers.

This cheered Elly up, and she was looking forward to the Thursday race meeting. It was before the time that racecourses supplied drivers for the vets. One of Steve's jobs was to follow the convoy of doctors, ground staff and vets who assist any casualties whilst competing there in races. Her main job for the day was to assist Steve around the track so that he could concentrate on not driving into the ditch between the course and tarmac road, and she would spot and assist him by carrying medication to any horse which had fallen at the fences. Not only did the vets carry potent painkillers but also Oxygen which was sometimes vital for tired horses which had fallen.

Elly also had an interest in the local racing yard which had an entry. It was the yard that also had given her Grace as a foal. They had many home-bred youngsters who had successfully made it to the race-track. During the week, Elly had the opportunity to analyse a blood sample to see if this horse was fit to race. She loved her laboratory work, and the samples would come through the door via the vets for not only National Hunt entries but also many Point-to-Pointers too. Elly had been taught by the late Roy Davidson, a founder of the practice she worked in, on how to look at samples down the microscope and do a total count on if a horse was responding to a viral and bacterial infection. The pressure was on, as some trainers would think that their horses were training well, but if the blood sample for white cells is elevated it could mean that the horse has a bacterial infection. This was often a lung infection and could sometimes only be detected on an endoscopic examination, for which some horses would need a sedative for. This obviously is against race rules, so they would only be sedated if absolutely necessary. Some horse's would take an endoscopic examination of their upper airway without sedation, but it is still a risk. Equally if the horse has a low white blood cell count it could mean that they are responding to a viral infection, which means they would be a poor performer, and probably would end up getting tired quite quickly during the race. Blood samples can also detect how rich the blood is too on red cell counts and haemoglobin level. Many trainers take samples when their horses are running well to judge when is an ideal time to get maximum performance out of them for their owners.

On their way to the races Steve asked Elly "What time is James's mare running New Looker? The one we did the blood on this week Elly?"

"She is in the three thirty a maiden mares hurdle race, I hope she runs well, her bloods looks good." Elly replied.

"Lets hope she makes a good start to her career." replied Steve.

Once at the races Elly headed off to find her friends. Steve had to be at a meeting an hour before the first race, so they planned to meet in the paddock once the horses were in there. The only downside about Elly going in work mode was that she couldn't join her friends for a glass of wine. Some of her friends were there to watch their horses run, or with syndicates when they had a small share in a horse.

"Never mind Elly, we can always get you a drink after the last race, especially as we have a runner in it." mentioned Sue, one of Elly's mates.

Elly enjoyed the racing just as much if she didn't have a drink as if she did, so all she hoped is that all horses came home safe and sound. The afternoon was uneventful, until it was 'New Lookers' race. Elly had placed a little bet on her each way, as she was hoping the mare would do well. She knew that the mare would maybe need the run, but the mares were equally rated in the race so she had a decent chance. Steve was following the horses around the course and in the home straight New Looker looked to be travelling well and in the first three. Then one of the three tumbled at the fence. The mare had just taken a false stride and the jockey was thrown down too. Steve stopped his truck and they headed towards the horse. Elly grabbed the treatment bag and Oxygen and stood to the side of where the groundsmen had put up the screens.

"I think she is just winded, Elly you give her some Oxygen please whilst I monitor her heart rate." Steve asked.

Elly placed the plastic tubing in the mares nostril and turned on the Oxygen. One of the assisting groundsmen was gently kneeling on the mares neck so that she didn't attempt to get up too soon. The idea is to keep them down until they are settled and hopefully they then get up and stay up. Steve checked all her limbs and was happy that the mare hadn't injured herself.

"OK all move to the side now, I think she is ready to stand up." Steve advised all, and the mare stood up with Steve holding onto the reins, which he then passed to a member of the groundstaff.

The screens were taken down and everyone breathed a sigh of relief. It isn't always good news but in this case the mare had just been winded. They all jumped back in their vehicles and the mare was lead back too the stables by her groom who had turned up to see if she was ok.

"I wonder if New Looker won the race?" Elly said to Steve as whilst they were busy looking after the fallen mare they had no idea who actually won the race.

Back in the paddock Elly could see that New Looker had gone into second place, apparently there was only half a length in the finish. She was able to pick up her betting money which paid out place form for each way which she had a couple of pounds profit.

Chapter Eighteen

Elly heard the news that she had finally passed her Equine Nursing certificate. She was thrilled and the team at the practice got together in the local pub, The Exeter Inn to help her celebrate. It hadn't been easy, and she had failed originally on one paper which she had to re-take. The main exam including the practical's were held at Cambridge University, which was a long distance from South Devon, Elly had hardly slept and her mind had been a bit scrambled to say the least. She had been gutted to fail on one paper, but was relieved that the tutors allowed her to re-sit her exam at Bristol, which was much closer to home. She was grateful to her bosses that they had allowed her to take the course, which in a mixed practice also had its challenges and distractions.

"I've a job for you Elly, we would like you to organise the next Equine Client Evening at the White Hart." explained Steve.

"Ok, that sounds like a challenge." replied Elly.

She was always up for a challenge, and to knuckle down and get the job done was her main focus. She listed her ideas down to show the boss.

1. Book venue
2. Book speaker and choose subject
3. Contact reps of drug companies for sponsorship/raffle prizes
4. Choose a charity to donate to
5. Draft invitations
6. List clients to invite
7. Choose buffet menu

She chose her moment to pin the boss down to discuss

the points with him.

"Good list." said Steve "Choose a day of the week when I'm not sailing, so not a Wednesday please." he asked.

"No problem." giggled Elly " How about Mr Darcy for the speaker?" she suggested.

"Yes I am sure he will pull in the horsey girls." laughed Steve. Mr Darcy was a clinician at Langford Equine Hospital, and being quite a dish and good at his job, they both knew he was an ideal candidate to ask.

"Ok Elly, you get a message to him, then we can approach the drug representatives for sponsorship. I am sure if we say we have Mr Darcy as a speaker on lameness, then they will come on board." Steve went off on his daily visits, leaving Elly to crack on and make the phone calls.

Elly had previously had the pleasure of helping Mr Darcy at Langford during an orthopaedic operation which Mr Darcy had done on a horse named Whatcanisay, which Steve had sent up there. She enjoyed making the call.

"Hi Mr Darcy, we are holding an Equine client evening and wondered if you would be able to come along and do a presentation on lameness for us please?" asked Elly.

"It would be my pleasure." came Mr Darcy's reply.

Elly blushed and giggled "Great, thank you. See you on the 20th." she replied.

The charity which they decided to raise funds for was World Horse Welfare, and Mr Darcy had been keen to support them too. Elly found it no problem either when phoning around to the representatives of drug companies, who all offered to donate raffle prizes to help raise funds for World Horse Welfare.

When Steve arrived back from his visits he was pleased with the progress Elly had made. The draft invitation was sent off to the local printers in Kingsbridge, and all was set for the meeting on the 20th. Elly drafted a list of clients on their books to invite, with Steve adding a few extras who he knew would be interested even though they hadn't a horse at the time, but he thought the more the merrier with it being a charity event too. They were sent out first class and already the replies were coming in thick and fast. Elly's close friends Lilly, Sara and Rachael were equally excited about the evening as they too knew how dashing Mr Darcy was.

The client's evenings are really good for PR for vet practices. Not only arranging a social gathering of like-minded people who loved catching up and chatting about their horses and ponies, but also as an opportunity for the clients to meet any new young vets working within the surgery. Equine owners are really fussy about who treats their animals, and rightly so, the older vets hold on to their good reputations and can be in high demand Whilst the younger vets are keen, have recent knowledge of any new drugs and treatments taught to them by the colleges they have just graduated from, but can lack some years of experience.

Over 120 people turned up to listen to Darcy's presentation. The evening turned into a great success. Elly had got Heather, another nurse, to help sell the raffle tickets which raised hundreds for The World Horse Welfare Charity. The prizes had varied from boxes of chocolates to smart rugs donated by many of the drug companies. Mr Darcy had not charged for his time, but was presented with two bottles of finest wine from Steve. It had been a busy evening for all the team with trying to give their time equally to all the clients questions and time. A tasty buffet feast was served by the staff at the White Heart, ensuring nobody went hungry.

Elly somewhat made a rod for her own back.

"You did really well in organising that event last night Elly, well done." Steve was pleased with the result and continued "You can do another one next month for the farm clients."

"OK." replied Elly. She knew that although it was hard

work, she enjoyed the result, and also having a good rapport with the local farmers, she would look forward to that evening too.

"Oh I have another job for you too." Steve announced and continued to explain.

"You like your laboratory analysis, well I've come up with the idea of a promotional worm egg count for our clients." He smiled "Tell me more?" Elly asked "Two for the price of one." Steve explained"Ok." replied Elly cautiously.

And she had the right to be cautious about the idea. As much as she liked spending time analysing samples in the laboratory, she hadn't realised just how much poo would be flying through the door, which kept her in the room with the potently smelling samples for over a week. Great idea, not!! She thought.

Chapter Nineteen

Elly was enjoying a lovely summer evening barbeque and wine with PK and Amy, when Amy asked Elly if she would like to be a pony judge at the Summer Yealmpton village show.

"We are looking for a judge for the lead rein and first ridden competition, and wondered if you would like to do it Elly? Amy asked her, adding "We know you have bred some lovely ponies."

Elly blushed and nearly choked on her glass of wine. "Gosh the Yealmpton Show is huge, and I know the quality of ponies which are shown there. Not to mention the colour co-ordinated mothers and children who have been around the County show circuit."

"You'll be fine Elly, you can come and have lunch with us in the president's tent after your class." PK giggled.

Whether it was the glass of fine wine that had affected Elly she will never know, but she replied.

"OK, I will be delighted and honoured to do it, as you know I love ponies, and can sure handle the mothers too I hope."

Amy acted as one of the secretaries dealing with the trade show exhibition, the show was held in July, so Elly had a couple of months to prepare herself for it.

Once in work the following day, Elly told Gail the practice receptionist what had been asked of her.

"Oh you will be fine Elly, you love ponies and can tell a good specimen against a bad one, but remember, you have to be fair. If one puts a foot wrong you cannot keep it high in the line, as it's not fair on the others." said Gail.

Elly trusted Gail, she acted like an auntie to her and she knew Gail had wisdom.

"Well I've agreed to do it, and PK has offered me to have lunch with them in the Presidents tent too after judging which will be fun." smiled Elly.

Yealmpton Show is always held at the end of July, and sometimes the weather can turn wet for a while. Elly was trying to choose her outfit for the day, and she narrowed it down to two. One with waterproof boots and wax jacket with also a wax hat, the other more summery, a light blue floaty dress, sensible flat shoes and a blue wide brimmed summer hat to match the dress. She was hoping the weather would stay fine. And that is exactly what it did.

She arrived early and reported into the secretary's tent. Elly was chuffed to see her name in the brochure which she was shown. She met up with Amy.

"You look lovely and very professional Elly." Amy gave Elly some encouragement.

Elly was then introduced to her class steward Rebecca, who she had never met before.

"Hi Amy, I'm Rebecca and will look after you today." explained Rebecca.

"Nice to meet you Rebecca, I hope I do a good job at judging for you." replied Elly.

The class before Elly's to judge was a driving class, and the lady judge in there seemed to be taking a long time.

"It looks as if we will have a delay Elly, It's gonna be more like another hour before we are ready for you." Rebecca suggested Elly take a look around the show whilst she was waiting. For Elly, dressed up, she was reluctant to go too far, and had a coffee and watched the driving classes, which brought her back memories of her trip to Hungary. By this time her stomach was starting to churn.

Several people had walked by, and on recognising Elly,

they complimented her on her outfit and said they would watch her judge her classes. This made Elly even more nervous. She was well relieved when it was her turn to stand in the middle of the ring, albeit an hour late. There was added pressure then as the other ring stewards wanted her to play catch up and not take too long.

One by one the first lead rein ponies were led into the arena. Elly noticed the quality was exceptional. All competitors had made an effort to colour coordinate their outfits to match the young jockeys on top. Even the Exmoor pony had turned out nicely and didn't look out of place coming up against the stunning little part-bred welsh riding pony types in there too. Elly asked her steward to line the ponies up in any order and do an individual show for her. She spoke with all of the child riders and asked them their ponies names and tried to put them at ease. Elly had her eye on one particular welsh bred pony who looked exquisite and reminded her of one of her own bred ponies Enya.

At this time she was aware that she had to hurry up and not take too long deciding. There were about ten in the class and she was keen to make sure everyone had a prize, although there were on rosettes to sixth place. Fortunately she had put together some goodie bags from work, which included a present from the drug companies being some fun leaflet booklets on pony care, a brush for them, a thermometer and a packet of polos. This made her feel better when awarding out the prizes. The black Welsh pony which she had noticed was her obvious first place choice. As they left the arena the crowd applauded.

"Did I do OK? Elly asked Rebecca.

"Yes you were spot on I think, and they all loved the treat bags." Rebecca smiled and organised the next class to come into the arena.

This was a first ridden class, where the parents do not

lead the pony in for the children, but they ride the pony in themselves.

Some beautiful ponies again! Elly thought and one by one they entered the arena. This time there were only six. Phew they will all get a prize, but in which order? Elly tried not to panic, she took a deep breath and got on with the job.

One of the pretty ponies decided to do a little rear as it walked into the arena. Elly saw this, and it could be tricky if trying to decide if it was a winner or not. No child's pony should rear, it's too dangerous. The pony then seemed to behave, and all the ponies were asked to walk, trot and canter around the arena before being asked to come into the line in any order.

Rebecca the steward asked the riders, on their beautiful ponies, to come and stand out in front of Elly the judge one by one. At this stage Elly was keeping open minded as to who she liked the most, but her heart wanted the naughty pony to behave himself as he was quite stunning. In the line also was one of the local ponies belonging to one of the practices clients. Elly hoped that this pony would behave too, so that she could award them one of the first three prizes on offer.

The first to come out was a little chestnut mare ridden by a young girl who also had red hair in plaits. She asked the young girl to do her show and watched them closely from the middle of the ring. The show wasn't perfect but good enough to be taken note of, and Elly whispered to her Steward.

"Can you note a 3.5 out of five please?" Elly asked Rebecca

The next pony was a very naughty grey pony with a young boy riding. When Elly had asked them to do their show, the grey pony was reluctant, and the young boy was flapping his leg to get any enthusiasm out of the pony to break from a trot into canter.

Once again Elly asked Rebecca to log the result.

"Only a 2.5." Elly pulled a face at Rebecca without anyone

seeing. Rebecca nodded.

Next out was the flashy pony which Elly liked but had noticed had a small rear as it napped it's way into the arena. Elly talked to the jockey, a young girl who was looking unhappy.

"Just do your best." Elly said as the young girl looked worried the pony would rear again. She felt sorry for the pony, which looked as if it cost a fortune, but was having its young rider on by being naughty. The pony again reared, but the young girl managed to encourage it forward and then did a beautiful show.

One by one the other ponies were presented to Elly and all did nice shows. Elly then discussed the results with Rebecca and the results were called out.

First prize went to a super little bay pony which had done a beautiful show with a smiley young girl jockey. Second went to another bay pony with a young lad who had performed a nice show. The chestnut mare was third with her redhead plaited jockey. Fourth prize went to the local lad on his pony who were clients of the practice. Fifth prize went to the beautiful black pony which although Elly liked, had been naughty in rearing, with sixth prize going to the lazy grey pony.

On leaving the ring Elly had hoped that she wouldn't be set upon by the mother of the child on the black pony, but it was the opposite. The mother came up to Elly and apologised for the pony being naughty, and explained that the pony was new to them and they hoped that he just needed to settle in with them. Once again Elly had given all of the entries a treat back, and this may be helped with them accepting their results.

Elly looked in the President's tent for PK and to have lunch, but due to the late start of the class, she had found that she had missed lunch, although desert was on offer which she readily enjoyed. To cap the day, Elly was able to join in on the judging of the championship for Best In Show and to her delight, the stunning little lead rein pony which she had placed first in her class was awarded reserve champion.

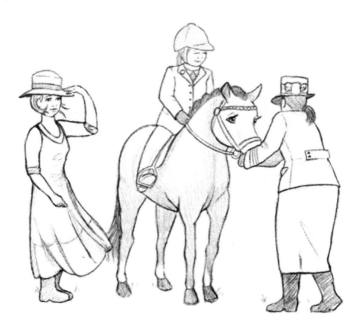

Chapter Twenty

Having enjoyed travelling to Point-to-Point horse races with Lilly, Elly had got to know many people on the racing circuit throughout the Devon & Cornwall area. Owners, trainers and grooms, along with the many talented jockeys who were riding in the amateur sport. Many clients of the practice, where Elly worked, had either shares in these horses or owned them outright, and many trained them. Some were local farmers who had a couple of Pointers in their yard as their hobby, and Elly would love being able to analyse their horses blood samples before racing. It became a passion of hers, as did following the young horses, some of which she had been involved with either at foaling, or assisting with castration of the colts. Then one day Lilly, who was the main press release office in the area at that time, asked Elly.

"How would you like to take on my PR job for the Point-to-Points Elly? She then added, "You have assisted me for a while and I am sure you could do it, I am just so busy with all the National Hunt journalist work, along with my other marketing work I really am struggling to find the time." Lilly explained.

"Gosh, do you think I am up to it?" replied Elly.

"You will be fine I am sure, I will help you to start with and be your editor so that you don't publish any rubbish." Lilly was keen to hand the job over to Elly as she had taken a lot more work on, and had her young toddler Timmy to look after.

"Ok I will give it a go, as long as Gary and Fred are cool with it." Elly replied Gary and Fred were the secretary and chairman, who were in charge of the area, and she would also work alongside Jack who already did the reporting. It was just the Previews which needed covering.

"They will be fine, I will let them know. They already know you and they will be pleased that I have found someone to pass the work on too." Lilly knew Elly would be ideal.

Elly knew the job would be a challenge, but she was up for it. The entries for the race meetings are not released until the Monday evenings. Some newspaper deadlines are the day before the entries are released, on the Sunday evening, when she would need to draft an introduction, but not make it look like an advert. Thankfully most of the secretaries for each meeting, of which there are about 26 every season, place their own adverts, so the newspapers are keen to support them in the What's On event page. Once the entries are released, she would need to do a meeting preview and include the entries. Although National Hunt racing and Point-to-Point entries are a week before, the Point-to-Points do not close until the day of the meeting, so you have no idea what will turn up to race on the day. It is a bit of a guessing game. Then, she not only does the newspaper version for a Tuesday lunchtime deadline, but also the website version for Wednesday morning. This can be longer and mention more about the horses entered, trainers, jockeys and anything which may attract a good crowd to the countryside event.

Elly enjoyed the challenge, at first it was daunting, Lilly was a perfectionist, and would go through Elly's Preview with a fine tooth comb. There would be some useful tips along with heated discussions, but Elly got there in the end with Lilly's help. Then there was the added worry of Have I chosen the winning horses? What will the racegoers say if I can't pick a winner? As long as the punters get a run for their money and the horses go well. She thought. However getting her name in print was a fantastic feeling. Not only in local papers, but also in some of the national racing papers and on racing websites.

She would never forget the first meeting of the season when Elly had provided her first racing preview. It was at one of the old courses at Black Forest Lodge, near Exeter, and she was nervous to say the least. One perk of being a press release officer is that an area car pass is given, to enable free entry to the course. On arrival Elly introduced herself to the secretary in one of the tents at the event.

"Hi Elly, would you like a racecard?." Linda greeted her to the event which made her feel at ease. Linda added "Do feel free to pop into our hospitality tent for a cup of tea or coffee during the day, and thank you for your lovely Preview."

Elly smiled "Thank you very much, I hope you have a good day and have plenty of runners and a good crowd." Elly had been pleased with the publicity that the newspapers had given the event. Being the first fixture of the season it's always tricky to tip winners, as many horses may have run well last season, but fitness could be an issue first time out. As for picking winners of the maiden races, which is for horses never to have won a race, Elly had gone by the advice from Lilly which was "Just pick a few out on names and mention breeding, as maidens are a minefield!" So Elly had been fair in mentioning some locally trained horses which she knew, and some outside raiders, who always would descend on the course and had a good record of stealing the prizes with their talented horses. Also local young jockeys, along with the previous years champions.

The day went well, much to Elly's surprise she had tipped three out of the seven winners and also three had gone close and punters were able to pick up money for a place. The two races Elly had failed to pick a winner were in the maiden races, which she had been warned by Lilly were the tricky ones. A good crowd had attended the meeting which pleased the organisers. The course had been beautifully prepared by the local Chanin brothers, and all the horses and jockeys came home safely. The only worrying comments which Elly received for her preview were from one of the bookies who she knew.

"Hey Elly, don't get too good at this game and tip all the winners!" teased Dave.

Harry also teased Elly about her tips. "You will have to keep this up now and tips some winners every week." he laughed. It was also Elly's job to act as a backup for Harry as he was to do the reporting at the events. Harry had been doing the job for years, was passionate about it, and knew his job well. Elly was proud and pleased to be working alongside him.

Chapter Twenty One

Having passed her trial with writing for the newspapers on the first Point-to-Point meeting, Elly was chuffed with her initial success. The team at the practice were pleased for her too. Not only did some of their clients own and train the horses, but also they acted as duty vets at four of the locally held meetings. Two at the Buckfastleigh course and two at Flete Park, where they provided the whole team of vets. It was Elly's job to help and assist at these, not only in gearing up each vet with the first aid equipment for them to use on the injuries if there were any on the course, but also to assist them on the days there. She found at that stage that she had a problem. Her heart was in the horses and racing, but she had spent the previous few summers and winters sailing on Sundays.

That summer she had been lucky enough to compete in the Round The Island Race, which was a large regatta held around the Isles Of Wight. Elly had sailed the 32ft Jeanneau to the Hamble with the skipper Roger. It was a fantastic experience for her, as Roger would leave her at the helm whilst he checked the navigation system and route. They stopped overnight at Poole, before heading up through the New Forest to meet the rest of the crew. They had spent a few days competing in their class and made really good progress with placing, but didn't win a class. Roger had recruited a mainly girl crew on his boat, much to the envy of many of the other competitors, but sometimes the girls lacked the strength to be really competitive if the wind blew. In one class the legendary Lewis Hamilton had competed, but the wind was so strong that his boat had dismasted before the finish. The girl team chuckled as they believed they had beaten Lewis in a race, even though he wasn't in their class. They drank to that, the boat had a good fridge containing plenty of fizz for the trip back to the pontoon after each race had finished, which they all enjoyed.

In the Autumn, the Icicle series started in Plymouth yacht haven. This was another venture which Elly sailed in, however the race days were on Sundays, so she needed to decide on horse racing or boat sailing. The decision became easy for her, as when competing in the annual Dartmouth regatta, she experienced a really bad day. As usual she helped Roger take the boat up a few days before the event, just the two of them and the wind had been lively enough.

"I think it's gonna be a really windy week, the forecast is not looking good." explained Roger as he appeared from below deck, he could see Elly was struggling to keep hold of the helm to steer the boat, so took over.

They didn't sleep at all overnight, as the wind blew strongly. Amanda, another crew member arrived the evening before too, and the girls discussed their worries over supper, whilst Roger had a meeting with the stewards in the yacht club.

"Elly your boss Steve is joining the boat tomorrow too, he will help with muscle and weight." Roger was trying to pacify the girls.

In the morning at breakfast the wind was blowing a force 6, and was forecast to rise to gusting 7. Elly mentioned her concerns to Roger. She really was a fair weather sailor and Roger knew that. But Roger just snapped at her.

"Don't be a wimp, you will be fine." he said grumpily.

"Fine, I will get my stuff, I'm off." Elly walked back to the boat, got her stuff and headed back over the river on the ferry. As she got off the ferry on the other side, she saw Steve, her boss.

"Where are you off too?" Steve asked "I just can't do it,

I'm totally shattered, haven't slept and the race shouldn't go ahead. It's too windy." she explained in tears.

Steve sympathised with her before jumping on the ferry towards the yacht club. Elly had phoned a friend who picked her up to take her home. It was Lilly, who fully understood how Elly had to give in. Once back at home the girls enjoyed some wine, which helped drown Elly's sorrows. They later checked the results on the sailing for the day, and unsurprisingly the racing had been cancelled for the day. Steve phoned to see how Elly was in the evening.

"Don't worry Elly, we sailed all the way to the start and one of the boats in our class was dismasted, so they cancelled the event." he explained which cheered her up. Fortunately no-one was seriously injured, but someone could have easily fallen off the boat, or got knocked off with the uncontrollable boom which held the sail. This became a deciding factor in Elly's decision, horse racing it was to be.

Elly settled back into writing previews for the newspapers and websites on Point-to-Point horse racing. She had passed her initial meeting, and the next event was scheduled to take place at The Royal Cornwall Showground at Wadebridge, in Cornwall. On looking through the many entries, she spotted a really good race to talk about in the being the Ladies Open. A really good horse called Byerley Bear was entered, he had won twice at the track before and looked like a course specialist, which she couldn't leave out. He looked to have some hot opposition this time though, with an ex National Hunt horse called Gwanako, who had previously won a race at Aintree along with other wins which had gained him a high rating and winning earnings of over 240 thousand pounds. It looked to be a good race and hopefully made an interesting feature to talk about in the papers and help draw in the crowd on a cold December day. Gwanako was now in training with a lady called Rosy who worked for one of the leading National Hunt trainers, she trained her horses at her home during her lunch breaks. This time Gwanako was to be ridden by the daughter of the National Hunt trainer as her first ride in a Point-to-Point at the start of her racing career. Elly thought it must be worth heading the feature about Maggie's first ride. She was really chuffed when the Western Morning News had used a picture of Gwanako with her Preview, they always did a good spread for horses, racing, farming and sports features. She took this along with her to the event.

Once there, she received a few positive remarks on her feature in the papers and on the website, along with some teasing comments again from the bookies which made her blush. Whilst walking to grab a welcome cup of coffee from the hospitality tent, she meets the father of the young jockey riding Gwanako waiting outside the weighing room. Elly had never met him before, but introduced herself briefly, whilst handing him her copy of her feature saying.

"I understand it's Maggie's first ride today? I featured her and Gwanako in my Preview and thought you may want this copy to give to her. I hope she does well." Elly smiled.

"Why thank you very much, I hope she does well too." Frank replied and smiled back as Elly walked away. The race was a thriller between the two horses, Byerley Bear on this occasion wasn't to be beaten and scored his hat-trick of wins at the course. Maggie rode Gwanako really well and finished a creditable three lengths second, and this kick started her career of seventeen Point-to-Point wins, six of which were on Gwanako.

Chapter Twenty Two

The young thoroughbred filly called Grace that Elly and Lilly had taken on, was now growing fast. She was a three year old, and had been enjoying life with her paddock mate Jessica Rabbit, at Steve's place. Elly had use of the paddocks for house-sitting at the property. There were two six acre paddocks and a two acre turnout paddock for the horses to enjoy, which had good shelter from the westerly weather. They had been kept out in the fields as much as possible, with two decent size stables to use in adverse weather. There was also a good field shelter, not that the fillies wanted to use it much. Elly would check on them twice a day, when not there full time house sitting whilst Steve and his wife Jan enjoyed their holidays. Also being determined to make sure the paddocks looked good, Elly would pick up the dung every other day, whilst enjoying the fresh air of the countryside. It helped keep her fit.

The summer had been particularly hot and dry, with the files becoming a nuisance, Elly placed as much fly repellent on the horses as she could each day. The fillies were getting used to being handled, and she would also check them for any wounds which they may have sustained whilst out. The field was well fenced with mainly hedging and post and rail, so fortunately injuries were minimal.

On one hot day, Elly noticed that Grace had got her fly mask off. Maybe she had been rubbing her face with the irritation, but Elly had been worried about her runny eyes, and asked Steve to take a look.

"She seems to have an infection, you will need to put this eye cream in daily Elly. But do be careful not to scratch her eye." Steve at the time wasn't too worried and thought they had caught the infection in time. At first Grace was good to have the cream in her eyes, she would blink as it was applied, but did not seem to be bothered. Elly would place the fly mask back on her and watch for a whilst the fillies continued to graze the grass. But by day three she was worried again.

"Grace is rubbing again, I am not sure the cream is working?" Elly explained to Steve.

Steve had another look. "She should be getting better by now. Bring her into the stable and I will have a look with my opthalmoscope."

Elly bought both the fillies in and Steve took a look.

"I can't see any damage at this stage, try another ointment and we will check her again in a couple of days. It will also help keeping her in by day, and you can keep the fly mask off her, but do put it back on when she goes out at night, just incase the flies are still irritating late evening and early morning before you bring her in." he explained.

Elly followed his instructions, but by another 48hrs Grace looked in real trouble. Then as Elly went to catch her to bring her in she just stood there as if she couldn't move. On approaching her, it was evident that Grace couldn't see. Elly spoke to her softly and gave her a pat on the neck as encouragement, and Grace walked beside her as she was led into the stable. Elly called on Steve immediately. He had just got out of the shower and went straight to the stable to have a look.

"We will phone PK to have a look too, but think she needs to go to the Equine hospital at Langford for a specialist to help her out. I am afraid it's not looking good Elly."

PK came out to have a look too, and the vets both agreed that Grace needed to go to Langford. Elly spoke to Lilly and they arranged transport immediately up to Langford.

It was the girl's friend David who took Grace to Bristol,

he was one of their Point-to-Point race friends and was pleased to help. After about half an hour they managed to pursued Grace to load onto the trailer. Her paddock mate Jessica Rabbit had travelled in a horse trailer before to get to the yard,so she was taken along as a companion and so that Grace wasn't scarred being short sighted and alone. Steve had given Grace some pain relief, which would also help her for the journey which would take about an hour and a half.

Once there Elly was directed to the specialist vet surgeon on the day Henry. She had met Henry before when attending the Equine Conference, and also when she had been at Langford to assist Darcy with the thoroughbred Whatcanisay's operation on his fractured hock.

"Hi Elly before we get Grace off the trailer and admit her to the hospital, please can yo give me your history on her." Henry asked.

"It came on really quickly, from what appeared just to be runny eyes from fly worry, to full on infection, swelling and what appears to be loss of sight in both eyes." She continued "Grace had a really bad start in life, she was three weeks and premature, couldn't stand at birth and was given to us by the stud farm where she was bred." Elly explained.

Henry could see that Elly had already been through a lot with Grace, along with her friend Lilly, they had done well getting her to this stage.

"Had she had colostrum at birth?" Henry inquired.

"Yes, she had been given four hourly feeds by the stud. She couldn't stand and the owners had milked the mare and fed her from the bottle. We then did a blood sample on her to check her serum IgG antibody level " replied Elly.

"Ok that's good, let's see how she walks as we get her off the trailer and then examine her in the box." Henry was calm and reassuring.

He could see that by goose-stepping off the trailer, she

could not see very well. They led her into the examination box where Henry sedated Grace so that he could have a good look in her eyes. The team around Henry, his vet students, nurses and assistants were equally compassionate.

"Right, I can see she has an infection and I will take a swab so that we can find out what it will respond to. We can also insert catheters into both eyes with a long delivery line to enable the medication can go into her eyes from a distance." he added "She also looks to have a uveitis which affects the middle layer of tissue in the eye wall, this may just be the inflammation, but is why her vision is affected."

So that was the plan. Grace stayed in Langford hospital for two weeks. She had catheters placed in both eyes, and responded well to the treatment which Henry had put her on, he hadn't waited for the swab test to come back, but chose an alternative therapy to the one she had been on which he thought should work. The staff at the hospital were great with Grace, they treated her every four hours at first. It took two of them to start with she needed help and was good, but as she became better she was a monkey to treat and had to have Acepromazine sedation tablets in her feed to keep her manageable. Poor Grace had been through a lot already in her three years of life.

Before Grace was sent home Henry phoned Elly to update her on the fillies progress.

"Hi Elly, Grace has responded really well to her treatment of Chloramphenicol drops. We have taken one catheter out, but have left one in as I think she needs longer treatment. Are you happy to have her home and do that?" he asked .

"Yes I am happy to carry on with the treatment, she will be at Steve's so he will oversee it no problem." Elly was relieved that Grace had responded to treatment.

"Oh one other thing, we took a couple of radiographs of her fetlocks, which you were worried about, and it was a good opportunity to use her as a study for our students. You will be pleased to hear we found them to be pretty normal, so you did well on the splint supports Elly." Henry said pleasingly .

"Oh thank you so much, that is such a relief for us to know. She may make it to the racecourse yet." Elly smiled.

THE END